Fallen From Other Skies

Tabitha Ormiston-Smith

DEDICATION

For every child who dares to dream.

CONTENTS

ACKNOWLEDGMENTS

My grateful thanks are due to Wendy Butler, who wanted to be in a book, and to Patti Roberts, for her wonderful cover designs and lasting friendship.

❧THE SECRET SUMMER OF PETER FOTHERINGAY☙

❧CHAPTER ONE☙

FROM: Carlina Fotheringay
<Carlina@redcarpet.net
TO: admin@TarringtonBoys.org.au
DATE: 19 December 2016 at 08:14
SUBJECT: Peter

Dear Mr Bamford,

I'm ever so sorry about the short notice, but Carthania is having some kind of tiresome political thingy, and Jack can't get away, so I'm afraid we're going to have to leave Peter there over the holidays. Perhaps you could give him some extra homework, or something? I'm sure he won't be any trouble.

Kind regards,
Carlina Fotheringay

FROM: admin@TarringtonBoys.org.au
TO: Carlina Fotheringay <Carlina@redcarpet.net
DATE: 19 December 2016 at 08:19
SUBJECT: re: Peter

Dear Mrs Fotheringay,

As you are no doubt aware, the summer holidays commence the day after tomorrow, and I am afraid it is out of the question at this late stage to arrange to board your son over the long break. The school will be closed over the summer, and he can hardly stay here on his own. Kindly make arrangements to have him collected.

Yours faithfully,
Bartholomew A. Bamford,
Headmaster

FROM: Carlina Fotheringay
<Carlina@redcarpet.net
TO: admin@TarringtonBoys.org.au
DATE: 19 December 2016 at 08:49
SUBJECT: re: re: Peter

Dear Mr Bamford,

Please, please don't say you can't help me out. I'm at my WITS END!!!! Surely someone on your staff could stay there over the Christmas break? A maid, or something like that? Peter is very self-reliant, and you could set him some extra homework or something to keep him busy. Anyway, there's just nothing I can do at this point. He'll have to stay there. Of course, we understand there would be an extra charge.

By the way, how is the fund-raising going for the new wing?

Must dash – horribly tedious cocktail party at the embassy. Do let me know how you get on.

Kind regards,
Carlina Fotheringay

.

FROM: admin@TarringtonBoys.org.au
TO: housekeeping@TarringtonBoys.org.au
DATE: 19 December 2016 at 08:50
SUBJECT: Houston, we have a problem

Dear Wendy,

I'm sorry to ask it of you at such short notice, but that awful Fotheringay woman has dumped her son on us through the Christmas break. Can you possibly stay and take care of him? You didn't have special plans, did you? I don't suppose he'll require a lot in the way of care, and there'd be a substantial bonus for you.

Cheers
Bart

FROM: housekeeping@TarringtonBoys.org.au
TO: admin@TarringtonBoys.org.au
DATE: 19 December 2016 at 10:20
SUBJECT: re: Houston, we have a problem

Barty,

You've got to be kidding. It's the SECOND LAST DAY of term. I'm counting the minutes, and most of the domestic staff have already gone. Anyway, I've got a cruise booked.

Wendy Butler
Housekeeper

FROM: admin@TarringtonBoys.org.au
TO: housekeeping@TarringtonBoys.org.au
DATE: 19 December 2016 at 10:32
SUBJECT: re: re: Houston, we have a problem

Wendy, please help me out. I can hardly take the boy home with me. You know how Helen gets with her nerves, and a twelve-year-old rushing about might bring on another attack. All you'd have to do is feed him and look after his room. You could probably teach him to do his own cleaning and laundry.

Bart

FROM: housekeeping@TarringtonBoys.org.au
TO: admin@TarringtonBoys.org.au
DATE: 19 December 2016 at 10:35
SUBJECT: re: re: re: Houston, we have a problem

Barty,

Sod off.

Wendy Butler
Housekeeper

FROM: admin@TarringtonBoys.org.au
TO: housekeeping@TarringtonBoys.org.au
DATE: 19 December 2016 at 10:36
SUBJECT: re: re: re: re: Houston, we have a problem

If you do this for me, you can have the gatekeeper's cottage. I know you've had your eye on it.

Bart

FROM: housekeeping@TarringtonBoys.org.au
TO: admin@TarringtonBoys.org.au
DATE: 19 December 2016 at 10:36
SUBJECT: re: re: re: re: re: Houston, we have a problem

Alright, you've got a deal, as long as I can move in immediately.

Wendy

FROM: housekeeping@TarringtonBoys.org.au
TO: J&PButler@coolmail.com
DATE: 19 December 2016 at 10:36
SUBJECT: Christmas plans

Dear Mum and Dad,

I'm really, really sorry, but I won't be able to go on the FiveStar with you after all. Something's come up at school and they need me to stay. There's a poor little boy who's been dumped here over Christmas. It breaks my heart to have to miss out on the cruise, but I know you wouldn't want me to leave a poor little kiddy to have Christmas by himself.

Love,
Wendy

FROM: housekeeping@TarringtonBoys.org.au
TO: Myfanwy999@coolmail.com
DATE: 19 December 2016 at 10:37
SUBJECT: Hallebloodylulia

Hey Miffy,

Result! At the LAST MINUTE, a CAST IRON EXCUSE came up to get me out of that dreary bloody cruise with the olds. THANK GOD!!! And you won't believe what else I'm getting. Maybe you can get over for a weekend after Christmas. I'll have plenty of room to put up a guest in my FLASH

NEW DIGS!!!!

cheers,
Wendy

FROM: admin@TarringtonBoys.org.au
TO: Carlina Fotheringay <Carlina@redcarpet.net
DATE: 19 December 2016 at 11:08
SUBJECT: re: re: re: Peter

Dear Mrs Fotheringay,

I have been able to arrange for our housekeeper,
Mrs Butler, to remain over the Christmas holidays
to take care of Peter. Please find attached schedule
of charges.

Yours faithfully,

Bartholomew A. Bamford,
Headmaster

FROM: Carlina Fotheringay
<Carlina@redcarpet.net
TO: admin@TarringtonBoys.org.au
DATE: 19 December 2016 at 12:16
SUBJECT: re: re: re: re: Peter

Dear Mr Bamford,

You dear, kind man! Somehow I just knew I could
rely on you. Give my love to Petey and tell him I'll
see him just as soon as these silly foreigners stop

shooting each other. I'm sure you can explain it all to him ever so much better than I could.

Kind regards,

Carlina Fotheringay

CHAPTER TWO

The suitcase wouldn't close, and Peter swore under his breath, throwing his whole weight onto the lid. He could hear the tap, tap, tap of Mrs Butler's heels coming along the corridor. She'd make him take everything out and fold it properly, for sure. He knelt on top of it and leaned over to force the catches closed just as the door squeaked, and had just time to jump up and look innocent before she swept into the room.

'Ah, Peter. Mr Bamford would like to see

you in his study.'

Peter ran a swift mental inventory of his recent misdeeds. Had Thompson blabbed about their late-night raid on the kitchen? No, it couldn't be that; she'd be in a furious bate, and she actually looked almost as if she felt sorry for him. A whisper of unease brushed against his mind, but he shook it off. Mum would be here any minute, and then he'd be on his way to – tada – Carthania! Land of exotic spices and old-world charm. Well, exotic cheeses, anyway. He'd read it up on Wikipedia. Carthania was famous for its cheese, and as far as he had been able to find out, for nothing else.

Farty McBumface, as the headmaster was known to the boys, was seated behind his huge desk. The lean, dark face gave no hint as to his mood; he always looked sour like that. Peter tapped on the open door and advanced across a daunting expanse of Turkish carpet. It was getting rather threadbare, particularly in the spot right in front of the massive desk. Must be where the expression 'on the carpet' came from. All the boys who had stood there, being barked at not to fidget, to get told off by Farty, over the years, had left the traces of their collective foot-shuffling.

'Ah, Peter. Sit down, sit down.'

Peter had a bad feeling about this. He sat on the edge of one of the leather chairs in front of the desk. He had never sat down in this room before. Any experiences related to the buttocks had had more to do with the thin, black cane, which rested in its little ring attached to the side of the desk. It was, he knew, a whip rest, meant to hold the driver's whip in a horse-drawn carriage. He'd found this out at an exhibition of vintage cars to which Aunty Jean had taken him last year. He hadn't told anyone, though. Peter liked secrets.

Farty ummed and ah-ed, shuffling papers and grunting.

'Fotheringay, I have received a communication from your mother,' he finally got out.

Peter couldn't think of anything to say to this, so fell back on the all-purpose 'Yes, sir,' being careful to maintain his aspect of carefree innocence.

'It seems – that is to say, there appears to be some level of political and domestic unrest at present in, ah, Carthania.'

'Yes, sir.'

'Your mother feels it would be safer for you to remain in Australia for the time being.'

For a few seconds, the words were mere noise, conveying nothing. Then their dreadful import slammed into him.

'The time being, sir?'

'Ah, hum, quite. Yes, I am afraid, my boy, that you must resign yourself to remaining here for the Christmas holidays.'

'What – the *whole* holidays? Sir, you don't mean the whole six weeks?'

'I am very much afraid so, my boy. Of course, it is possible that, should the situation in Carthania improve, your mother may make arrangements for you to travel there for the latter part of the holidays. But you would be unwise to rely on such a thing. Hah. Hum. Most unwise.' He paused for a few moments, shuffling among his papers.

'Now here,' the Headmaster continued more briskly, 'is a list of suggested reading for your holidays. 'You should find all of these books both enjoyable and instructive.'

He held out a sheet of paper with what Peter supposed was meant to be a genial expression.

'There, my boy. Chin up! It's not all bad, you know. Lots of quiet time for reading. I expect to see you top of your form next term.'

'Thank you, sir,' said Peter, taking the paper. There was a lot of writing on it. He sighed.

'You will find all of those in the school library. Now of course the library will not be attended during the holidays, so I am placing you on your honour to leave everything exactly as you find it, and not to take out more than your allowed two books at a time, understood?'

'Yes, sir.'

'Now Mrs Butler has kindly agreed to remain at school to take care of you. I'm sure I need not tell you not to make things more difficult than necessary for her. I expect you to offer to help her whenever you can. It's the decent thing to do, the gentlemanly thing, understood? See if you can help her in the kitchen, with the housework, that sort of thing. She'll be moving into the cottage, so you might also see if you can help her with anything there.'

'Yes, sir.' It was getting harder to keep up the easy politeness the Head demanded. Peter groaned inwardly, envisaging days spent as an unpaid skivvy and nights wading through acres of dim old books. He backed out of the headmaster's office, waiting until he was safely in the corridor before contorting his face into a horrible grimace.

Peter sat in his room with the door closed, glaring at Parker's bed, which had already been stripped, the brown school blankets neatly folded across its foot. All along the corridor, he could hear doors slamming and happy cries of farewell as the other boys, one by one, were called for by parents and left Tarrington for the beach, for town, for exotic foreign holidays. Murchison was off to California, to visit his cousins who had a ranch there. The Fitzpatrick twins were going to Kenya for a wildlife safari. Until yesterday, he had felt comfortably superior. Everyone knew what America was like from television, and Africa was common too – there were so many documentaries about it. Carthania, though, Carthania was *special* – mysterious for its very obscurity, and he had been going to be the only boy in the school who had ever been there, and besides, he would have been staying at the embassy, which was way cool. He had, he realised uncomfortably, rather put on side about it. If only he'd shut up.

As the day wore on, the happy shouts of departure became fewer and less frequent, and by five the school was silent. He could hear the ticks and creaks of the building as it settled into the late afternoon, hunching down like a great stone animal, composing itself for sleep. Even in the quietest hours of the night, he had never before heard such a deep, absolute stillness in the school. It came to him with a queer little shiver that he might now be the only person left in the whole building. He imagined himself wandering the corridors, the school's last inhabitant, isolated as a marooned sailor on a desert island, no one knowing or caring about him. The thought was pleasing in its melancholy, and he sat for a while, turning it around in his mind.

And then, in one of those sudden shifts of

perception that turn the pattern of cubes from concave to convex, or reveal the Grecian urn to be nothing but a pair of human faces in profile, he saw, instead of loss, opportunity. The deserted school, waiting to be discovered in all its complex secrecy. His loneliness, turned on its edge, now freedom, absolute freedom to go where he would, to explore the 'off limits' parts of the old house. There might even be a secret passage; in fact, the more he thought about it, the more certain he was that there had to be something of that kind. Old houses in books always had them. Tarrington Boys' Grammar School, he knew from the prospectus, had been the residence of a wealthy squatter, built in 1862. No doubt there would be all kinds of secret nooks and things, in case of a convict uprising. There might even be hidden treasure! And whatever he found, he vowed, he would not tell anyone. The knowledge would be his, his alone. He'd start first thing tomorrow.

He descended the stairs to dinner in a much

happier frame of mind.

The huge, cavernous dining hall, now dim in spite of the remaining hours of daylight with its brown Holland blinds drawn, was strangely unfamiliar. Peter's footsteps echoed as he moved hesitantly to his usual place. The effect was creepy and offputting. When he heard Mrs Butler call through the serving hatch, he jumped a foot.

'Is that you, Peter? Come on through, we might as well have dinner together in the kitchen, since it's just the two of us.'

More relieved than he cared to admit, Peter stuck his head around the door. Coming into the kitchen from the gloomy wasteland of the hall, he blinked, the light from banks of fluorescent tubes striking him at first like a blow. He had never been inside the kitchen before – the midnight raid he'd perpetrated with Thompson didn't count; then, it had been Enemy Territory, the frail circle of their furtive torch casting only enough light to find their way to the left-over treacle tart, the whole thing removed by the hour and the occasion to the world of fantasy and make-believe. In normal time, he had only had glimpses of it through the serving hatch, and it had always seemed a fast, bustling place, filled with steam and clattering and uniformed, hair-netted kitchen staff rushing about. Now, ranks of stainless steel stood silent and inert.

Mrs Butler had set one end of the long table for two. Peter sat nervously. It felt funny, having dinner alone with a strange lady. He didn't really know Mrs Butler as a person; she was the housekeeper, and he'd often been told off by her for running in the corridors, leaving his bed unmade or failing to wipe his feet when coming inside, but they'd never had what you might call a conversation. Being told off wasn't a conversation, because you never said anything back. 'Yes, Mrs Butler' didn't count; you weren't really saying anything when you said that. It was more like a dog sitting when given the command.

Dinner was chops, with mashed potatoes and green beans. It was standard school fare, but as they ate, Peter restraining himself from his usual gobbling in deference to his company, Mrs Butler kept up a steady stream of talk, all about food. Did he like Italian food? How did he feel about sushi? What was his favourite meal? Encouraged, Peter informed her at some length about his culinary preferences, which in his two years at Tarrington Boys' Grammar had never been of the slightest interest to anyone.

Dinner over, he leapt to his feet, and was about to dash off when another thought struck him. In order to pursue his investigations, it would be best if he really were alone in the house. Mrs Butler had, he knew, an uncomfortable habit of appearing when least expected, materialising from around corners as if the brisk tapping of her high-heeled shoes could be muted at will, allowing her to operate in stealth mode.

He knew she was moving into the old cottage, because Farty McBumface had said so, and if he played his cards right, perhaps, just perhaps, she could be induced to stay there most of the time, leaving him the freedom to ramble unmolested.

'Let me do the washing up,' he said, face shining with innocence.

'Oh, you don't need to do that, Peter. It's my job, remember.'

Peter assumed what he hoped was an expression of grave morality. 'Mrs Butler, I know you're giving up your own holiday to look after me. It's the least I can do.'

'Well, alright then. Thanks. Anything you don't know where it goes, just leave it on the table and I'll put it away in the morning, when I come up to get your breakfast.'

'Well, about that, Mrs Butler, I was thinking, I could easily get my own breakfast every morning. Then you wouldn't have to come up from the cottage.'

'Really, Peter? Are you sure?'

'Course I'm sure. It's just pouring out a bowl of cereal and some orange juice. I'll clean up after and everything. My aunty never used to get up before ten, so I always got my own breakfast at her house.' He sent up a mental apology to the shade of his departed aunt, a lifelong early riser and firm believer in the nutritive power of a cooked breakfast.

'Well, if you're sure…'

'Absolutely.'

'Alright then, I'll see you tomorrow for lunch. Now, mind, lights out at nine. Just because you're on your own, that doesn't mean you ignore school rules.'

'No, Mrs Butler.'

෨CHAPTER THREE෪

Peter washed up very carefully, wiping every surface and hanging up the dish towel to dry. It was no part of his plan to have his newfound kitchen privileges revoked. The evening stretched ahead, massive and unbroken. It was the first time in his life he had ever been really alone.

He was tempted to start his explorations right away, but it seemed wise to hold off for the first night. Mrs Butler, he thought, might take it into her head to check on him, so it behoved him to be in bed on time; the 'lights out' was purely notional, of course, as at this time of year it wasn't really dark before ten-thirty. Instead, therefore, he headed for the library.

The list the headmaster had given him was quite long, but when he sat down and actually looked at it, he found he had already read quite a few of the books. That was a bonus; he had no doubt Farty McBumface would remember the list and quiz him on it after the holidays. He ran down the list. *The Lion, the Witch and the Wardrobe*, check. *The Secret Garden*, check. *The Jungle Book*, check. *The Hobbit*, check. Good lord, he'd read all those back in primary school. Did Bumface think he was a baby?

He ticked off everything he'd read. Good, he was already six down. Surely that had to be good for a couple of weeks? He scanned the remainder of the list, which was still depressingly long, and after looking up a few titles, settled on *Animal Farm* and

Watership Down. Peter liked books about animals. He had been trying to convince his parents to let him have a dog for years, but the response was always the same: who would look after it all the time he was away at school? It wouldn't be fair to the puppy, etc. In vain he had argued in favour of remaining at whichever embassy his father was posted to and attending a local school, marshalling argument after argument about multiculturalism and early fluency in a second language, but always the answer was the same: his father and grandfather had both attended Tarrington Grammar, and he would therefore attend Tarrington Grammar, as, it was hoped, would his sons and grandsons, *ad infinitum.*

He took the books up to the junior common room, but found its empty tidiness oddly oppressive; even when he turned on the television, the absence of the other boys made the friendly, relaxed common room feel somehow *wrong.* It wasn't *supposed* to be empty; either it was full of other boys, or you weren't supposed to be in there. In the end he retreated to his own room, to sprawl on his bed in forbidden luxury, and read about rabbits until the distant chiming of the hall clock recalled him to the danger of discovery, and he scrambled hastily into his pyjamas.

For the first couple of days, Peter roamed the building, paying special attention to areas that were out of bounds. These were the staff quarters, the headmaster's flat, and the staff common room. The staff quarters were not of great interest to him, consisting as they did chiefly of other people's bedrooms. Having spent most of his life at boarding school since he had turned seven, he had had little enough in the way of privacy himself, and he shrank from invading those most private of spaces.

Farty McBumface's flat, however, he considered fair game. He did not think of the Headmaster quite as a person, but rather as a thing of nature, and his flat seemed to Peter to be something like a fox's hole – to be treated with caution, but warranting investigation. It was, therefore, with some chagrin that he discovered the door to the flat was locked.

'What have you been doing with yourself all morning, Peter?' asked Mrs Butler, setting before him a plate from which a heavenly smell arose.

'Oh, just reading, you know. Mr Bamford gave me a list of books to read in the holidays. I'm reading *Watership Down*. It's awesome.'

'Well, mind you get some fresh air. Have you been outside at all?'

'Not really. It's too hot.'

'Well yes, there is that. How do you like this? It's Scallopini alla Romana.'

'It's very nice, thank you,' said Peter,

shovelling it in.

'I thought,' Mrs Butler went on, shaking out her napkin, 'you might like to come down to the cottage for Christmas dinner. You do realise it's Christmas Eve tomorrow? In my family we always have our main celebration on Christmas Eve. Will you join me for that? We'll decorate the tree and play some Christmas carols.'

Peter put down his fork, suddenly not as hungry as he had thought. He hadn't heard from his parents at all, and the reminder that it was Christmas Eve tomorrow brought a lump to his throat. He had been expecting to celebrate this Christmas at the Australian embassy in Carthania. There would have been snow. The loss of the snow, so exotic and wonderful to an Australian child, hurt him more than not seeing his parents. Of course, he loved his mother and father, he told himself, although in fact he hardly knew them; apart from occasional holidays at one or another foreign embassy, where he was largely in the care of staff, he had lived with his aunt for the five years since he had been sent away to school, and his parents were not a part of his life, not even as much as Mrs Butler and Farty McBumface. Still, it stung to think they had not even sent him a present.

'Thank you very much, Mrs Butler,' he said carefully, swallowing the lump. 'That would be very nice. I don't suppose,' he went on, 'there's been any mail for me?' Mail during term time was brought to the front hall and distributed by the form captains.

Mrs Butler froze, fork poised halfway to her mouth. 'Oh, you poor boy!' For a horrified moment, Peter was afraid she was going to get up and hug him. 'I completely forgot you'd be expecting something from your parents, of course you are. It's just that normally, you know, I'd be away too, so it's not part of my routine to get the mail. It all gets put into the box down at the gate and I haven't been down to clear it. I'll tell you what,' she went on, 'we'll walk down there together as soon as we finish lunch.'

Spurred on by anticipation, Peter bolted the rest of his food, and declined pudding on the grounds that he was already full. They washed up together, Peter washing and Mrs Butler drying, and when the counters were all wiped down Mrs Butler disappeared into her office across the hall, emerging with something in her hand that froze Peter in his tracks.

'Wow,' he said, forcing down his excitement, trying to sound casual. 'That's a mighty bunch of keys.'

'A housekeeper's burden, Peter. They weigh a ton.'

'Gees,' said Peter. 'I bet you must have a key to every door in the whole place.'

Mrs Butler appeared faintly surprised. 'Well, of course.'

Peter could barely refrain from skipping as they walked down to the gate. All he had to do now was get his hands on them.

There was, in fact, a biggish, flat parcel

addressed to Peter, bearing the distinctive Carthanian postage stamps, which were large and featured Friesian cows. He could feel, though, that it was a book of some kind. Still, at least they hadn't forgotten him. And now, the more exciting part of the walk. His heart beat faster as he turned to Mrs Butler.

'Geez, it's so hot. Would you like me to take those keys back for you, Mrs Butler? Save you the walk?' Say yes, say yes, he silently urged. His whole body tensed as he strove to impose on her mind the feeling of being hot, of being tired, of not wanting to walk any farther than her own cool verandah, perhaps of even wanting to soak her feet, privately, in a bucket of cold water, as Aunty Jean had sometimes done in the worst heat of the summer.

'That's very kind of you, Peter. Do you know where they go?'

'Um… sort of.' It wasn't really a lie. Every schoolboy knows that 'sort of' means 'not at all'.

'There's a hook on the wall behind the door of my office. Good boy. You can take the rest of the mail up while you're at it. Just leave it all on my desk, and I'll sort it out when I come up to get dinner.'

'Rightio. Catch you later, then!' He was away at a dead run, hoping his haste would give the impression of keenness rather than the fear she'd change her mind.

Once in the cool, echoing front hall, he dropped the letters and his parcel on a table and examined his catch. There must be thirty or forty keys there, but he saw with relief that many of them had little tags.

It was now shortly after half past two by the big grandfather clock in the corner. He had, he estimated, a clear two and a half hours before Mrs Butler would be coming up to cook dinner. Perhaps longer, but certainly not less. He took a moment to rip open the parcel, carefully folding the paper with its cargo of Carthanian stamps, which could be traded to Dobson for his collection, in return for some homework done. Dobson was very good at Maths.

A small huff of disgust escaped him as the book emerged from its shroud of brown paper. *Birds of the World.* He flicked through the pages. It was all pictures of birds and information about birds, dry facts he could easily find on Wikipedia, if, that was, he were at all interested in birds. He sighed and tossed the book back on the table. Mum never had any idea.

Quite a few of the keys could be eliminated right away. Those to the several outside doors, for example, were of no interest to him. They were all on a separate ring attached to the main ring, and he slid it to one side, tucking it out of the way. That left two other rings. One bore such labels as 'gdn shed', 'sports pav', 'pantry', and 'inf cbd'. He hesitated for a few moments over Inf Cbd, but decided that pills and bandages were of no real interest. It was secrets he wanted, after all, not illicit drugs.

The third ring was far more promising. It bore upwards of a dozen keys, each labelled only with a pair of initials. These, he reasoned, had to be the staff's private rooms. He had already considered and rejected these as a possible target, but among them, oh, among them was the treasure he had sought – the label 'B.B.'

✂CHAPTER FOUR✂

The habit of caution around the Headmaster was hard to overcome, and Peter found himself tapping gently on the door, and then knocking more loudly, before daring to use the key. Suppose Bumface was there? He knew, of course, that he couldn't be, but just suppose! He could say… he'd think of something.

There was, however, no reply, and after drawing a few deep breaths of courage, he inserted the key in the lock.

There was nothing very special about Old Bumface's flat, as far as he could see. Peter tiptoed across to the window and opened the curtains. In the remorseless glare of the afternoon sun, the room was revealed as a large, rectangular space, furnished in a formal style, with several glass-fronted bookcases and a nest of solid, massive chintz armchairs surrounding a low table. At one end of the room was a rolltop desk, its cover down. There were a number of dark, grubby-looking pictures on the walls. A door next to the desk led into a bedroom, also large, gloomy and old-fashioned. Opening off it was a private bathroom.

Some time later, Peter was startled by the sound of the hall clock striking five. Oh, help! He had lost track of the time as he prowled furtively around the flat, peering into drawers and poking behind books in the bookcase. He closed the door as quietly as he could and raced downstairs, breathing a sigh of relief as he saw the book and the pile of letters and *Birds of the World* undisturbed where he had dropped them in the hall. He scooped them up and ran to Mrs Butler's office, his heart pounding wildly as he heard the big front door creak open, and the familiar tap-tap-tap across the hall. The nail was a little farther over than he'd expected, and he hadn't time to do more than hang up the keys and toss the letters on the desk before she appeared.

'Oh, hello, Peter! Were you looking for me?'

'Um, yes. I was.' What else could he say? He should have vacated her office hours ago.

'Something you wanted?'

Peter's heart sank into his sneakers. 'Um, I was wondering… um… I thought perhaps I could help you make dinner. I mean, see, Aunty Jean was going to teach me to cook, and now she's gone….' He felt bad about using his dead aunt, but needs must where the devil drives, as she'd always said herself, and he supposed she wouldn't grudge it in a good cause.

Mrs Butler melted. 'Oh, you poor little lamb. Of course you can help me. We're having Spaghetti Bolognese. That's a nice easy dish for you to start on, and it's a great one to have in your repertoire. Come on and wash your hands and we'll get started. Is that the book you got from your parents? *Birds of the World*? Lovely!'

As he dutifully chopped garlic and a couple of chillies, listening with one ear to Mrs Butler prattling on about the many ways Bolognese sauce could be varied, Peter hugged to himself the knowledge of the one discovery he had made, had stumbled upon quite by accident when he idly opened the Headmaster's bathroom cabinet. The secret worked itself into a little jingle that ran in his head:

Farty McBumface dyes his hair
Farty McBumface dyes his hair
Dyes his hair and his beard, oh yeah
Even dyes his hair DOWN THERE

At this point he sniggered, startling Mrs Butler, who had been holding forth with some passion about the merits of fresh, as opposed to dried, basil, and had to say he had been laughing because the basil had made him think of Fawlty Towers, of which his aunt had been so fond. Aunty Jean seemed to be getting him out of trouble on an hourly basis, he mused. Perhaps it was really true that the spirits of the dead looked out for those they'd loved in life. He made a mental note to take some flowers to her grave when he should have the chance.

It was not until Boxing Day that Peter was able to resume his explorations. Christmas at Mrs Butler's cottage had been more fun than he had expected, and had gone a long way to relieve his loneliness; prompted by his mention of *Fawlty Towers*, Mrs Butler had, after a sumptuous roast dinner, produced a DVD of *Monty Python and the Holy Grail*. They had enjoyed the film, helped along by several glasses of non-alcoholic cider, which

Mrs Butler supplemented by adding vodka to her own glass. On Christmas Day, she had surprised him by appearing in the morning to bear him off for a day out at the nearby bird sanctuary, displaying a startling knowledge of birds. She had, she said, known he'd like it because of *Birds of the World*. She wasn't such a bad old stick. He enjoyed the day out, and lunch at McDonald's, which, he knew, would have brought his mother out in hives at the very thought.

He was up with the dawn on Boxing Day, his head full of plans. Today would be the day, he just knew it, the day when he would discover something wonderful. He didn't bother with a shower; he'd had one yesterday, anyway, and there was no point wasting water, he told himself virtuously. There was no point wasting water washing a glass either, so in the absence of adult supervision he downed a long draught of orange juice straight from the bottle, and ran his cereal bowl and spoon briefly under the cold tap before replacing them in the cupboard and drawer.

The business of the morning over, he turned his mind to his project. He had already exhausted the possibilities of the Headmaster's quarters, and felt at a bit of a loss, so he decided to walk right around the whole interior of the building, looking for anomalies. He was still very hopeful of finding a secret passage. Surely, in a house as old as this, there must be something of the kind.

The ground floor drew a blank; kitchen, offices, laundry room, dining hall, library and classrooms. The first floor, more classrooms and the science lab on one side, and the staff quarters on the other, separated by a massive door, yielded nothing either. By the time he climbed the stairs to the second floor, where the boys' rooms, the little kids' dormitory and the form common rooms were located, he was starting to wonder if the whole idea was a dud. But he had determined to go over every inch of the house, and that was what he would do. He wandered up and down corridors, looking into a myriad of small, stark bedrooms: two boys per room except for the Remove, which housed six boys in each room, in bunk beds. Everything was very plain up here, compared to the panelled walls and richly carved embellishments of the lower floors. It must originally have been the servants' quarters, he thought.

When he came to the door, he almost failed to see it. It was right at the far end of the West corridor, where the senior boys' rooms were, and there was a bookcase in front of it. The nearest window was back in the middle of the building, where the staircase emerged from the first floor, and what light filtered down here was faint and paltry; the small dead end of the corridor was sunk in gloom, but barely visible above the top of the tall bookcase was something that looked very much like the top of a door.

It took him half an hour to unload the books into piles, and then to move the bookcase out. It was indeed a door, he saw, inwardly shouting with exultation. He tried the handle; it was stiff, probably rusty, but with a bit of effort, it turned, and the door swung outward.

On the other side was a tiny space, just big enough to accommodate a staircase that led steeply up. Peter could see a faint light from up there. Hardly daring to breathe, he set his foot on the stair.

At the top of the stairs, he paused and looked about him in wonder. He was at one end of a vast, open space; it must, he thought, be the whole top of the house. An attic. He'd never even heard that there *was* an attic. It must have been forgotten, the knowledge of it lost, perhaps before the house had even been made into a school.

The richness of his find overwhelmed him, and he stood for a few minutes where he was, gazing at the sea of jumble that filled the vast, dusty space. There was not a great deal of light; what there was came from large but grimy windows, spaced rather far apart and almost opaque with dirt. In fact, everything was covered in dust. He'd be covered in it himself before very long. He'd better be careful; Mrs Butler was sure to smell a rat if he presented himself for lunch wearing the dust of ages.

His first priority, he decided, had to be escaping detection. It was fortunate that Mrs Butler, in their new-found camaraderie, had decided there was no point in trekking up to the school twice a day, and had told him he'd better come down to the cottage each day for his lunch and dinner. Still, he would need to be presentable, and also, he didn't want to be going through all that with the bookcase twice a day. He descended the stairs and closed the door, taking stock. The end of the corridor was very dimly lit, and there was a gap of at least six or seven feet from the last pair of room doors to the end of the passage. If he moved the bookcase forward a bit, leaving just enough room to squeeze behind it, he didn't reckon a casual glance would reveal anything different. After all, had he not almost missed seeing the door himself? And anyone coming up here would be coming for a purpose, to clean or whatever. Yes, that was what he'd do.

As he shifted the bookcase, grunting with effort, he worked out the rest of it. He'd have his shower before going down for lunch, and after lunch he'd get back into his dirty clothes. He could repeat the process before dinner; it would mean two showers, but he wouldn't have to wash much the second time; all he'd need to do would be rinse off the dust. Would Mrs Butler notice his hair was wet? She probably would. She did have a knack of noticing anything one would rather she didn't, as, for instance, the time Parker had secreted a hoard of forbidden chocolate under his mattress. He'd been sprung before he'd even finished unpacking. It was as if she had x-ray vision.

So, the choice was between not getting in the shower and risking her noticing the dust, or getting in the shower and causing her to wonder why he was having so many showers… or, he supposed, he could wear something on his head. Yes, that was the go. He'd wear his school cap when he came up here. Then he could just wipe off his face, and his arms, and get back into his clean things, and he'd be good to go.

Pleased with his solution, he replaced all the books on the shelves and slipped behind the repositioned bookcase. The door banged against its back, and he wished he'd measured a bit more carefully, but he could still squeeze through sideways. He closed the door behind him and ascended into his new domain.

His heart sped up as he regarded his trove. Piles of junk were distributed haphazardly all over the vast space, some of them as high as his head. Old furniture, great wooden boxes filled with God knew what, lamps, a dressmaker's form, and hulking, amorphous shapes shrouded in sheets. Through an archway he could see into another section containing more of the same. It was like a junkyard, only without the garbage and broken glass. He moved through the islands, treading in narrow lanes between tottering piles.

There did not seem to be any plan to the way the attic's contents were distributed; Peter had rather the impression that things had been deposited higgledy-piggledy over many years. He had never seen anything approaching the sheer complexity of it, and he wandered at random, not knowing where to start.

<<FLASH>>

Peter blinked, his eyes watering. Something had dazzled him with a fierce light. He peered about, looking for the source of it.

<<FLASH FLASH>>

There, it was coming from over there, something in the next section, just past the archway. Something must be reflecting the sunlight, something very shiny indeed. He started to pick his cautious way in its direction, but just then he heard, remotely and very far away, as if underwater, the faint, shivering tones of the great hall clock, and as he waited, counting, he realised with a sharp stab of alarm that it was striking twelve.

❧CHAPTER FIVE☙

He showered in record time, dragging on clean clothes without drying himself properly, which slowed him down more than if he had taken his time, thrusting a comb through his snarled hair, wishing he'd combed it before getting under the water, and sliding down the bannisters, free of the watchful eyes of prefects and masters, almost overbalancing on the second slide but righting himself with a wrench to stumble to the door just as Mrs Butler opened it from the other side.

'Peter! Did you forget you were coming down to the cottage for lunch?'

Ah, bless her! She'd handed him his excuse.

'Yes Mrs Butler, I'm ever so sorry, I just forgot, and I looked for you in the kitchen and I thought you were just late, and then I remembered....' He kept chattering away as they walked down to the cottage, the blazing December sun mercifully drying his hair. That was something he hadn't thought of; at this time of the year his short hair would be dry in minutes, outside in the sun. The five minute walk down to the cottage would be enough.

The attic was suffocatingly hot when he returned after lunch. Up here under the roof, the temperature had to be in the forties. Sweat prickled down his back, and the thought of doing anything requiring physical exertion, even to the extent of moving stuff out of a pile, was not as attractive as it had been in the relative cool of the morning. He decided to circumnavigate the whole attic before settling on what to investigate first. Perhaps by the time he'd been right around he'd be acclimated.

It was actually a series of attics, load-bearing (Peter assumed) walls crossing the width of the long space, with big archways left in the middles. He picked his way cautiously between heaped-up furniture, the flotsam of years.

<<FLASH>>

He recoiled as blinding light stabbed into his eyes.

<<FLASH>>

There it was again, that painfully bright reflection.

<<FLASH FLASH FLASH>>

Peter changed course. He'd see what that was, and perhaps turn the reflective surface around a bit, because the flashing reflection was giving him a headache. It had seemed to be coming from a pile of stuff in the corner, there where one of the windows had been broken. It was probably a bit of the window glass reflecting.

He picked his way towards the broken window, careful not to topple anything from its precarious piles, until a sudden, overwhelming burst of light and colour invaded his brain and sent him crashing to his knees, blinded and floundering.

The brightness of it was beyond anything he had ever known, each flash an almost physical blow. He could no more rise to his feet than fly to the moon, and he crouched on the wooden floor, breathing the dust of centuries, while layers of purple and lime green exploded behind his eyes. He tried to cry out, all the time aware that there was no one to hear him, and that if he couldn't get out of this he would die here and his body would never be found, because he'd been so clever camouflaging the entrance to this place that it might be years and years before another boy discovered it.

The assault on his visual cortex went on and on, and Peter curled himself into a tight little ball on the dusty floor and moaned softly, the nearest he could get to a shout for help. He must be having some kind of attack: a stroke, or a heart attack. So this was what dying was like. In his mind he reached for the only real human comfort he had known in his short life, for the memory of Aunty Jean. He stretched, he yearned for the safety, the normality of her, and

<<FLASH>>

In an instant the violent, pulsating lights and colours in his head were – not gone, exactly, but in some strange and impossible way they were *changed* into a great, booming voice that echoed and bellowed in his head.

<<LEAVE THIS PLACE OR DIE, PUNY BEING>>

He was hallucinating, he must be, but as the afterimages cleared from in front of him, he relaxed the tight clenching of his eyelids and risked a glance towards the window, and saw that he was not alone.

Hunched on top of a pile of disintegrating old books, a creature sat, staring at him and clutching a small box.

<<I WILL END YOUR INSIGNIFICANT LIFE>>

It looked almost like a cat, he thought, his mind ricocheting from it to the booming voice, which continued to utter threats. Hands clamped over his ears, he stared at the creature in amazement. Creature, but not an animal; those were definitely hands that held the small box, which, he now saw, seemed to be some kind of electronic device, with different coloured knobs on its upper surface.

<<I WILL CUT OUT YOUR [burst of static] AND DANCE ON YOUR BONES>>

The creature itself, squatting atop the old books, did resemble a cat more than anything else. A Siamese cat, with its face and pointed ears, and its legs and tail, tinted the colour of milk chocolate. No earthly cat had ever had fur that colour, though, a delicate jade green mottled with faint striations of a darker shade. It was – it had to be, thought Peter with mounting excitement, from Elsewhere. An extra-terrestrial – or perhaps a dimensional traveller. His preference for science fiction over fantasy decided him on the former. A creature of magic wouldn't have a box with knobs. He sat up cautiously, his head still ringing with the overload of sound.

<<PREPARE TO DIE, FILTH SPAWN>>

Peter waved his hands in what he hoped was a placatory gesture. Evidently the creature spoke at least some English. 'Hey,' he shouted over the deafening threats, 'can't you keep it down a bit? You're hurting my head.'

<<I WILL DISINTEGRATE YOU INTO YOUR COMPONENT ATOMS>>

The creature, at his movement, had scuttled behind a large box that balanced precariously across two piles of junk. It glared out at him from this cover, conveying an impression of deep mistrust. Somehow, despite the threatening shouts, it didn't look very fearsome.

'I'm not dangerous, honest,' he went on. 'Please, couldn't you not shout quite so loud? You don't want other people hearing you.'

The creature narrowed its eyes and seemed to be adjusting something on the box, which, Peter saw, was slung round its neck on a narrow strap. The booming subsided to about the volume of an angry sports teacher on the football field. It was a great improvement.

<<DO NOT APPROACH, MONSTER, LEST I SLAY YOU IN MY TERRIBLE WRATH>>

Now that his senses were not being overloaded, and the throbbing in his head was almost down to a bearable level, Peter could see that the creature, whatever it was, seemed to be more frightened of him than he was of it. It was evident in the quick, flinching movements, in the way it ducked behind the box when he moved, peeping timidly round one end, its manner a strange mismatch to the bawling voice. The dissonance was so great that he wondered if it might be a recording.

Faced with the unthinkable, Peter fell back on the one thing that had never failed him. Politeness.

'How do you do,' he said. 'My name's Peter.'

<<I AM ZARKOZ THE MIGHTY, DESTROYER OF GALAXIES. FEAR ME, PUNY MONSTER>>

Okay, so not a recording, since it had responded to what he'd said. He ventured on another remark.

'Have you been here long?'

<<FOR MANY AEONS WE HAVE BEEN HERE. WE WILL BE HERE WHEN WE

HAVE DESTROYED YOU. FEAR US>>

It was all just a bit too dramatic. Stagey, somehow. *It's bullshit,* whispered a small part of his mind. *It's all a big bluff. He's frightened, more frightened than I am.*

'Don't worry,' he said kindly. 'I'm friendly. I'd never hurt a – well, anything.'

The box reminded him of something, and he recalled an episode of Doctor Who. It must be a translation device, he thought with excitement. The creature was definitely a Real Alien, and he, Peter Fotheringay, was making a First Contact. His heart swelled within him. He wouldn't let down the human race.

The voice had modulated itself somewhat. Now it was only as loud as a normal person talking, or not much louder.

<<Are you sure?>>

'Of course I'm sure. I'm from Melbourne. We're multicultural. We welcome all different sorts of people.' Mentally he crossed his fingers, thinking of the offshore detention centres.

The creature was still fiddling with the knobs on its device, and presently there was a – well, not quite a click; there was nothing audible, but it *felt* like a click, and Peter became aware of the absence of something, some discomfort or dissonance that, overborne by the dreadful lights and extreme sound levels, he had failed to notice. With this absence came a definite *presence,* a feeling of – well, of someone else, close beside him, so strong that he glanced to his left, half expecting to see another person.

The creature seemed more comfortable, too; it had stopped cowering behind the box and was now sitting on its haunches like a possum, long tail wrapped around its feet.

<<Game mode off.>>

❧CHAPTER SIX☙

The sun moved across the sky as Peter sat with the creature. He had quickly become used to the telepathic translator, once it had been properly adjusted. They talked about their worlds. Peter explained about Parliament, and agriculture, and the drought. Zarkoz the Mighty didn't have much to say about his world, other than that it was ever so much better than here and he wanted to go home.

'I say,' said Peter, after a while. 'Zarkoz the Mighty, Destroyer of Galaxies, it's a bit of a mouthful. Would it be okay if I called you Zark, for short?'

There was an odd feeling of turbulence through the translator, as if the sandy bottom of a clear stream had been stirred up with a stick, and was slowly settling.

<<Not Zarkoz! That's only for Game Mode. You can't play pretend in Real Mode, everyone knows that. It doesn't let you.>>

Peter digested this. 'So what *is* your name?'

<<Binky.>>

A thought occurred to Peter. 'So, Binky, how come you're here? It's not, like, an invasion or anything, is it?'

A feeling of embarrassment came through the translator, followed almost immediately by a wave of anguished longing that almost had Peter in tears himself. Binky wanted his mum.

There was a trick, he was discovering, to using the telepathic translator. You had to sort of hold onto yourself, so as not to be swamped by the other person's feelings. Probably people normally weren't as emotional as Binky seemed to be when they were using it. Probably they were all sciency and grown-up. Binky, it was becoming clear, was neither sciency nor grown-up.

'So, Binky, how old are you, actually?'

There was another little flurry of turbulence; this happened, apparently, when there was some difficulty in direct translation. Then he felt the knowledge in his mind; not a verbal translation, it was more abstract than that, but Binky's age in terms of his relative maturity. If Binky had been human, it turned out, he would be about six years old.

'Woah.' Peter was shocked and horrified. Poor little kid. Stuck here, on a strange planet, all by himself. 'What happened? Where's your…' he didn't want to say 'mother', in case it upset Binky too much. 'Where's your people?'

More turbulence, then a halting translation.

Something had gone wrong. They had been going on a trip for their work, Binky's mother and father, and they'd taken Binky along for a treat, because it was just a routine trip. It had been Binky's first time in space, and happiness and excitement washed through Peter's mind as he recounted it, tinged with a complicated kind of pride that he couldn't quite grasp. And he'd been exploring in the ship, and he'd got into the escape pod, just to see what it felt like, and he'd been playing with the controls, and the hatch locked itself and he couldn't get out, and the pod jumped out of the ship, and next thing he was here. And he'd been here for ages and ages… here the translation dissolved into a wordless wave of utter misery, to match the piping cries that Binky was himself emitting.

Peter picked him up and held him until the shrill cries diminished. Poor little bugger, he was just a baby. What were they thinking, he scolded to himself. What kind of idiot let a little kid run round a spaceship on his own?

Morons. He found himself rocking Binky, in the age-old instinctive action that humans use to comfort a small child. Presently, the translator settled into a stream of almost tangible peacefulness. Binky had cried himself to sleep.

He sat down carefully, still holding the sleeping child. He had stopped thinking of Binky as a creature, he realised, or even as an alien. Now he was just a scared little boy. Or girl. Whatever, but a small, frightened child. It was up to Peter, somehow, to make it all better, because that was what you did for little kids. You had to fix it when things went wrong for them, because that was what big kids, and for that matter grownups, did. That was Being A Person.

His first thought was to take Binky straight to Mrs Butler. Since he'd become better acquainted with the crotchety housekeeper, he had found a deeply motherly woman beneath the cross, pernickety exterior. She was kind, he knew, and had a good sense of humour, which usually went with not being too close-minded.

Something stopped him, though. Let's think about this, he told himself. Once you tell her, it'll be too late to think better of it then. It was the government that worried him. What if he told her, and she reported it to some authority or something? Look at what they were doing to the refugees, shutting them up in concentration camps which Aunty Jean had said were hellholes. And those were *human* refugees. What would they do to Binky? He wasn't sure it was safe to tell anybody.

There was also the question of whether he could adequately care for Binky until – until what, he asked himself. There had to be some kind of 'until', surely. Binky had come down in an escape pod, which he took to be the same kind of thing as a lifeboat. Lifeboats had emergency beacons, didn't they? Or flares and stuff. He'd seen it on the movies. You got clear of the sinking vessel, and then you sent up a flare when you heard the choppers, and they'd see it and come and get you. Surely a vessel as sophisticated as a space-going craft would have something like that? And where *was* this escape pod, anyway?

From downstairs, he heard the far-away hall clock strike five. He would have to go down soon; he needed to get back into his clean things and get to the cottage by six. But he didn't like to wake Binky, and he found himself unwilling to leave him, to have Binky wake up and find him gone; it seemed unkind. He stewed until he heard the clock strike the three quarters, then gently shook the sleeping child.

'Wake up, Binky. Wake up.'

Binky stirred fretfully and flung out an arm. 'Mummy?' Peter's heart sank. He didn't know when he'd felt so bad for anyone.

'Binky, it's me, Peter. I have to go away now for a bit. I'll come back, okay? In a couple of hours.'

At dinner, Peter was abstracted, and had to keep asking Mrs Butler to repeat what she'd said. He accounted for this by claiming to have reached a very exciting part in *Watership Down*. He made his escape as quickly as he could after helping with the dishes, and raced back to the attic, stopping only to ransack the pantry for anything he could give Binky to eat. He had forgotten to ask Binky about his diet, but based on the kid's appearance he felt he was almost certainly a carnivore; he really did look very much like a cat, if you ignored details like his hands and green fur. With the school closed for the holidays, there was no fresh food, but he found a big tin of corned beef and some sardines. He opened both tins, only cutting himself a little bit, and dished out some of each food into a soup bowl. There was still milk in the refrigerator, left for his breakfasts, so he poured a glass of that, and added a second bowl. He supposed Binky's escape pod must have had emergency rations, but he thought the food might comfort Binky, that even if he couldn't eat it, even if it was completely the wrong kind of food for him, just being offered it might be a comforting sort of thing.

He was no sooner up the stairs when Binky let loose with a flood of complaints and recriminations. Peter had left him alone when he wasn't properly awake. He was hungry and cold. The escape pod facilities needed servicing.

'Okay, okay,' said Peter. 'Keep your fur on. I brought you something to eat. See if you like this.'

Binky did like it. He buried his whole head in the bowl, with audible moans of ecstasy and a low-level feed over the translator that sounded oddly like *nomnomnomnomnom.*

The bowl licked clean, Binky sat up and announced that he was thirsty. He sniffed suspiciously at the glass of milk, and demanded to know what it was. 'Milk' didn't seem to translate very well, so Peter had to explain about cows and dairy farms.

This was not well received. The only coherent word Peter understood from the translator was 'Yuk', but it was accompanied by feelings of such roiling disgust that Peter came close to losing his own dinner. As he removed the offending glass and raced down the stairs to fill the clean bowl he'd brought with water, he wondered if he'd ever enjoy a milkshake in quite the same way again.

৯০CHAPTER SEVEN৪

Peter lay awake for a long time that night. He had offered to let Binky share his room, but Binky wanted to stay with his lifeboat. He seemed to have a confused idea that if he left it, his parents would never be able to find him. He hadn't liked to leave the kid on his own up there, but had salved his conscience by taking Parker's blankets and pillow up to the attic to make a cosy nest for him. Not that he could imagine anyone wanting a woollen blanket in this weather, but cats, Peter knew, did like to be warm, and Binky, whatever he was, did *look* like a cat. Sort of.

He woke in the middle of the night to a strange sensation. There was a rippling stream of contentment running through his awareness, and something soft and heavy was weighing down his covers on one side. He stretched out a hand, and felt cool, smooth fur. Binky had changed his mind about having company.

He sighed and lay back, staring at the ceiling. He was responsible for Binky now, alright, until he could be got back to his own people. God knew how he would manage once term resumed, if Binky was still around then. The trouble was, he was so very *young*. The same lack of caution and common sense that had landed him in his current predicament was bound to get him caught sooner or later, and Peter had a very bad feeling about that. And it was all very well to go 'yada yada First Contact', but Peter didn't think it counted as a First Contact when it was just a little kid.

Morning came too quickly, and found Peter tired, cross, and rather achy from having to sleep scrunched over to make room for Binky. Binky, curled into a ball with his head out of sight, still streaming that lull of mindless content, didn't stir when he pulled the blankets straight. He didn't worry about making his bed properly; he didn't believe Mrs Butler was all that keen to do extra work during the holidays, and so he had become progressively more relaxed about the state of his room, which indeed looked rather as though it had been tossed by burglars.

Binky was stirring by the time he came back from the kitchen, with more corned beef and an empty bowl for water, which he filled from an orange-juice bottle he'd salvaged out of the recycling bin. He greeted Peter with cries of delight and affection, which turned peevish as soon as he saw the food.

<<Want more shiny things.>>

Peter hadn't opened another can of sardines,

because there were not many in the pantry and he didn't want his thefts to be noticed. 'It's bad for you to eat too many of those,' he temporised. 'You might get sick. You can have more tomorrow, if you're still here.' Hopefully, he wouldn't be. Peter had some ideas about that.

While Binky was hoovering up the beef, Peter tried in a tactful way to ask him about toilet arrangements. His tact was unnecessary.

<<Got all that in the pod.>>

'Okay, well we can go back up there as soon as we finish breakfast. Um, where is the, um, pod?'

<<Stupid. You saw it.>>

Peter didn't recall having seen anything that looked like an interplanetary spaceship's escape pod. But then, he didn't know what one was supposed to look like, either. He'd find out soon enough, he supposed. His plan depended on it; he was relying on the basic similarity of function, and confidently expected there would be some kind of distress beacon that could be used to alert Binky's parents to his whereabouts. It stood to reason.

Binky insisted on accompanying him to the kitchen for his own breakfast, where he did his best to put Peter off by channelling his disgust at the milk in Peter's bowl of cereal. What was it about milk that was so bad, Peter wondered. Binky looked so like a cat, surely his people had to be mammals? Binky did accept a small bowl of orange juice, but left half of it and shook his whiskers, splattering sticky drops all over Peter and the table.

While he was washing up the dishes, Binky ran nimbly up the curtain and dropped on his head –

<<WHEEEE>>

– rebounding into the sink and splashing

water and suds all over the floor. Peter gritted his teeth even more, and reminded himself again that Binky was just a tiny kid, that he'd been alone for much longer than a tiny little kid should ever have to be, and that it would be mean to object to his high spirits. He reminded himself of all the times he'd wished for a little brother, and how he'd imagined taking care of the younger boy. It was pathetic if he got shitty after less than a day, he told himself sternly. He dried Binky off with four of the clean tea towels and tossed them in the hamper for the dirty linens, hoping Mrs Butler didn't count them.

It was with some difficulty that Binky was persuaded to return to the attic. He had seen the kitchen garden through the window, and wanted to go outside. In the end Peter carried him up all three flights of stairs, while being battered by angry protests, both audibly and through the translator. In vain he attempted to explain the need for secrecy.

'There's bad people,' he finally said in exasperation. 'They'd hurt you.'

<<You mean like [burst of static]?>>

Peter supposed the concept was untranslatable, but every world must have at least some criminals.

'Yeah, probably. Like that.'

Binky scrunched himself into a little ball.

<<WANT MY MUM>>

'Yeah, okay, calm down. That's what we're going to do today, figure out how we can get hold of your mum. Where's the pod you came in?'

Binky uncurled and shook himself. <<Stupid. It's right here.>>

'But where?' Peter couldn't see anything but junk.

<<Here, see?>>

Binky jumped to the top of the pile where

he'd first seen him. Then he hopped into the big cardboard box that was balanced on top of it. Was the pod in the box? Peter moved towards it, and as he came within touching distance a strange thing happened. The box seemed to become transparent, although in a way it was still solid, but at the same time, more distinctly as he moved closer, a gleaming metal ovoid, about the size of a child's pedal car or rather larger, occupied the same space. When he put out a hand to touch it, it felt faintly warm and somehow alive, as if a smooth machine hummed within it.

Binky popped up at one end.

<<Got everything. Food, toilet, everything.>>

'Well there must be a beacon to call the ship. Can you show me the control panel?'

<<What's a control panel?>>

'Where you make it go. Where you make it do things. Like on the translator, you've got those knobs, see here?' He pointed to the controls on Binky's translator box. 'Like that.'

<<Stupid. It's right here, see?>>

The front end of the pod, at least Peter supposed it must be the front end, did indeed have what looked more or less like a dashboard. There was a screen, now dark, and a bank of slider controls below it, with writing beneath each one. Of course, he couldn't read the alien writing. It looked a bit like Indian, he thought. He'd seen Indian on the fronts of restaurants.

'Binky, do you know what all these knobs do?'

<<That one makes food come out.>> He depressed a yellow button on the far left of the board. A brown pellet popped into a basket below it. Binky seized it and held it out to Peter.

<<[burst of static]. Very good. You have some.>>

Dubiously, Peter took the pellet and nibbled one end. It looked like chocolate, and had a similar consistency, but tasted like nothing on earth. With difficulty he restrained himself from spitting it out.

'Very nice. Thanks, but you have the rest. I'm not hungry just now. So, what do all these other knobs do?'

Binky paused to devour the pellet.

<<Don't know.>> He accompanied the remark with a strange, wriggling motion of his body, terminating in an expansive sweep of his tail. Peter supposed it was the equivalent of a shrug. <<Let's play [burst of static].>> He bounded away through the piles of junk.

'NO! Come back, we have to figure this out. We'll play later, we'll play whatever you like, okay? Come back here now and help me with this.'

Binky trotted back, tail waving high, looking almost impossibly like a cat, if you ignored the green fur. The fingers on his hands seemed to retract at will, allowing their use as feet. He sat neatly, tail curled around his paws, and looked at Peter with a confidence that was somehow annoying.

'Can you tell me what all these words say, on here?'

<<That one makes food come out. Want some more?>>

'No more food just now,' said Peter hastily. 'Maybe later. What does this one say?' He pointed to one of the legends.

<<Push back.>>

Retro-thrusters, Peter translated, having watched plenty of science fiction movies. 'How about this one?'

<<Push.>>

Okay, thrusters. This seemed to be working. 'And this one?' He indicated a horizontal slider with a word at each end.

<<Go left, go right.>>

'Good! This one?'

<<Blow up. KABOOM!>>

Shit! Self-destruct button, right out in the open. 'This one?'

<<Go home signal.>>

Peter could feel his face glowing in triumph. He'd cracked it! Then, he saw the problem. The two buttons were positioned side by side on the board. The two words were between them, one above the other. And he didn't know which word went with which button.

One button was white and the other green. The colours had significance, obviously; all the knobs on the panel were variously coloured. If one had been red, he could have assumed it was the self-destruct.

'Binky, listen. Which button is the blow up kaboom button?'

Binky leaned over the side of the pod, examining the dashboard with the air of one encountering something completely new.

<<That one. Or maybe that one.>>

'Great, thanks. That's a big help.' Peter wondered if sarcasm would go through the translator. Evidently not, for Binky bounced up and down, all happy, and a wave of pride emanated from him. *He's just a little kid,* Peter reminded himself. He racked his brains for another way to approach it, but nothing presented itself. Binky didn't know which was which, and that was that. If the knowledge wasn't there, you couldn't get it.

If only there were an instruction manual, one like you got with your iPod, with a diagram and arrows pointing to all the different bits. He could match up the diagram in the book with the controls on the console, and they'd be home free.

Binky had wandered off again. Peter leaned over the pod, examining its interior. There was the console, and in front of it, or rather behind it, a padded bench that was obviously the pilot's seat. Or the passenger, anyway.

Behind it was a metal box with a hole at the bottom. He supposed that must be the toilet. There seemed to be nothing else.

Peter sat down and tried to remember every movie he'd seen that had lifeboats in it. In *The Titanic*, he didn't think there'd been anything in them. In *Life of Pi*, however, there had been a big storage compartment, with heaps of emergency food, water, and equipment. And, he remembered with a surge of excitement, there had been a manual!

But however carefully he examined the tiny craft, both inside and outside, he failed to discover any storage compartments.

∞CHAPTER EIGHT∾

They spent the rest of the morning in the attic, playing Binky's game, which turned out to be Hide and Seek, and going through some of the junk, with Peter attempting to explain the purpose of various items. Binky didn't seem to understand the notion of clothing, but was fascinated by it, and coaxed Peter into putting on an old-fashioned dress, full of ruffles and lace. Peter felt like an idiot, but completely failed to explain about gender. Well, not gender as such, but the idea of men and women having different clothes.

<<You should wear this,>> Binky kept saying. <<It's pretty.>>

There was a problem when Peter said it was time for him to go to lunch.

<<Lunch! Goody!>>

'No, Binky, you've got to stay here. You can't let Mrs Butler see you, not ever, understand?'

<<Why?>>

'Well, because. There's bad people, I told you, remember?'

<<Is Mrs Butler a bad person? You should stay away from her.>>

'No, she's nice, but there's other people. If she sees you, she might tell them. You can't let her see you. Promise me. Anyway,' he went on, inspired, 'it's time for your nap.'

Struck gold! Yay for babysitting young Fiona last holidays. Binky grumbled a bit, but curled up in his nest of blankets willingly enough, and within moments appeared to be fast asleep, a wavery trickle of contentment filtering through into Peter's mind.

The telepathic translator had a limited range, and by the time Peter was on the attic stairs, his awareness of Binky had winked out. He had become so used to the constant feed of awareness that he felt a little bereft, but it was twelve fifteen and he had to hurry, and the rush of showering and getting into clean clothes left no time for thought. He covered the distance to the cottage at a dead run, presenting himself flushed and panting on the doorstep at twenty minutes to one.

Mrs Butler opened the door, frowning.

'I do expect you to be punctual, Peter. I know it's the holidays, but I have other things to do than wait for you.'

'Sorry, Mrs Butler. I lost track of the time. It's hard without the bells.'

Mrs Butler appeared to accept this, and Peter

followed her into the cottage, congratulating himself on a fine piece of weaselling.

His complacency lasted until midway through the meal, when a small, green head popped up in the window, and Binky scrambled onto the sill.

Mrs Butler was facing away from the window, but she was still looking at him, and so he couldn't even gesture to Binky to get away. Not that Binky would probably have understood a gesture, or obeyed it if he had. He could feel sweat breaking out on his forehead.

'Are you feeling alright, Peter? You look as if you'd seen a ghost.'

'Um. Yes, just a bit – actually, I think I might be getting a cold.'

Binky hopped down into the room and started to sniff at the sofa. Abruptly the telepathic translator cut in, sending a waft of satisfaction and pride into Peter's mind.

<<Ha, ha. Found you!>>

'I can't imagine where you could have caught a cold. Unless it was when we went out.'

'I expect it was that,' said Peter. 'It takes a few days to develop, doesn't it? I probably need to *get out* more, in the fresh air. How do you feel?'

'Fine…" She rubbed her forehead and gave herself a little shake. 'What's that you keep staring at?' She turned around just as Binky whisked behind the sofa.

'I thought I saw something moving over there, down on the skirting board. Might be a tarantula.' With satisfaction, he saw her flinch. Ladies were always scared of spiders. 'If you want to go out of the room, I could catch it for you. Put it outside.'

'I think it's much better to kill it,' said Mrs Butler firmly. 'There's no sense putting them outside, they only come straight back in again. Filthy things. I'll get the spray.' She left the table, going into the kitchen.

The instant she was out of sight, Peter rushed to the sofa.

'Get out, quick!' he hissed. *'She's going to spray poison under there. It could kill you.'* He reached in, grabbed Binky by the scruff and hauled him out, rushing to the window and leaning as far out as he could before dropping him into a freshly-turned flower bed. *'Now get! Back to the attic!'* He pulled himself back in, dropping to his haunches under the window just as Mrs Butler re-entered the room, bearing an economy size can of Mortein and shaking it threateningly.

'Move away, Peter, we don't want any of this getting on you.'

'I can't see it, Mrs Butler. I think I must have been mistaken.'

Nevertheless, she sprayed a choking cloud under and behind the sofa before resuming her seat at the table.

'So, Peter, you were telling me about the book you're reading, but what else have you been doing with yourself? I hope you're not spending your whole holiday buried in a book?'

There, he knew it had been coming. That grown-up obsession with fresh air and exercise, although they never seemed to be so keen on it themselves. What could he tell her? Something that she wouldn't be tempted to join in. Ah, yes.

'Well, I've been running laps around the oval in the mornings. Trying to get my speed up to try out for the Junior Eleven next term.' He affixed a look of sporting keenness to his face. That always went down well; teachers loved you to be keen on sport, and Mrs B, being school staff, was a kind of teacher.

'Yeah,' he went on. 'I go out real early, before it's too hot, see. Get in a couple of dozen laps before breakfast.'

Binky was nowhere to be seen when he came out of the cottage, and Peter hoped he had gone back to the attic, but he kept an eye out nevertheless, looking under bushes and up trees as he walked back to the school. But there was no sign of him, and when he mounted the narrow stairs, he found Binky curled up fast asleep in his nest of blankets, looking for all the world as if he'd never left. The giveaway was the translator feed, which instead of the dreamy content usual from a sleeping Binky, jumped and jittered with alertness and anxiety, with an undercurrent of sly satisfaction.

'Alright, you can stop pretending to be asleep. What did you think you were doing down there, eh? You'll get yourself killed. Killed dead, do you understand?'

<<Wanted to see. Wanted to see where you went. And I found you!>>

Peter sighed. There was no way to impress on Binky the absolute need for secrecy. He was a normal child in his own world, Peter reminded himself, just an ordinary little kid, of little interest, probably, to anyone save his own family.

Binky had stopped his feeble pretence of sleeping, and was rummaging through a box of trinkets that had been in the trunk of clothing. He held up a long earring, tiered drops of something that Peter was sure couldn't be real diamonds, but which sparkled and caught the light, casting tiny rainbows.

<<Pretty. Can I keep it?>>

In for a penny, Peter thought. After all, this junk had been abandoned for who knew how many years. Let the kid have it.

'Yeah, I guess. There ought to be another one in there.'

Binky raced back to the pod, somehow managing to run on all fours while still clutching the earring. Peter couldn't quite see how he did it. He leapt into the pod and, a moment later, popped back out, minus the earring, and resumed ferreting through the trunk, tossing out clothes and sundry items. On the brink of scolding him for making a mess, Peter bit his tongue. You'd never even notice the difference up here. He ought to get his own room picked up, he thought vaguely. Tomorrow was Wednesday; that was Sheet Day, and no doubt she'd be coming along with clean sheets and a clean towel, since there were no boys rostered to collect and distribute the linens. He needed to do some washing, too.

'Hey, Binky. I've got to go downstairs for a bit, you want to stay here or come with me?' After the lunchtime incident, he felt it was safer to have Binky under his eye at all times. He couldn't do much harm in the laundry room, surely.

His optimistic mood lasted while he gathered up all his dirty clothes, while he descended the two flights to the ground floor, dragging his bulging laundry bag, while he loaded his clothes into the machine and added powder. The long row of washing machines stood in neat silence, their lids up. On the other side of the room were the big tumble dryers, which were only to be used on rainy days, on pain of a conduct mark.

Tarrington Boys' had embraced the green way of life with a vengeance, although some people thought it had more to do with cutting costs than saving the planet. Peter didn't care; Aunty Jean had been a great believer in the sanitising power of sunshine, and in the summer heat everything would be dry in a couple of hours.

He selected his cycle and was about to close the lid, when

<<PANIC   TERROR   SHOCK DISASTER>>

He heard the slam of another lid and saw the lights on in a machine at the other end. Leaving his washing, he raced over and snatched up the lid, revealing a drenched and miserable Binky.

'What on earth were you doing?'

<<FELL IN. IT WAS ALL DARK AND WETTY. WANT MY MUM!>>

Peter sighed and carried Binky to the folding table. He rummaged about in the machine, which mercifully he had not closed, and found a couple of t-shirts, which he used to mop the worst of the water from the shivering, crying child. *Kids*, he thought, echoing his aunt. *Who'd have 'em?*

And then he heard a sound that chilled him to the bone. Along the corridor came the tap-tap-tapping of Mrs Butler's high heels.

'*Keep quiet and don't move,*' he hissed as he stuffed Binky onto the top of the machine next to his own. The raised lid should screen him from view. '*Turn the translator off, quick.*'

He swiped the t-shirts across the table, removing the telltale water, and tossed them on top of his load, just as Mrs Butler entered the room.

'Ah, Peter. Doing your washing?'

What was it about grown-ups, Peter thought savagely. They always popped up right when you wished they wouldn't, and they asked these inane questions. What did she think he was doing, holding a revival meeting?

'Yes, Mrs Butler,' he said meekly. 'Will I do my sheets and towel as well? It would save you the bother.' Offering to do something sucky, he had found, could nearly always divert an adult's suspicion.

'Yes, Peter, that would be great,' she replied absently, bending to peer at the table he had so hastily wiped. 'Come and look at this.'

His stomach sinking, Peter crossed to the table and looked where she was pointing. There, neatly marked in dirt, was an unmistakable pawprint.

&CHAPTER NINE&

'Gosh,' said Peter. 'It looks like a paw print.' He couldn't believe how stupid he sounded, but nervousness had seized him, and he just couldn't seem to stop. 'From a paw,' he went on, feeling sweat break out on his forehead. 'It must be some kind of animal. Maybe a possum.'

'It looks like a cat to me,' said Mrs Butler. 'Have you seen a cat anywhere about?'

'No, not me.' He shook his head frantically. 'No cats, not one. Are you sure it isn't a possum?'

Mrs Butler was adamant. 'No, a possum's prints are quite different. Longer toes, you know? This is definitely a cat.' She sniffed the air. 'I can't smell anything, can you?'

'Smell anything? Like what?'

'Well, like tomcat.'

'I don't know what that smells like,' said Peter.

'Well, are there any windows open on the ground floor? Did you open any, Peter?'

On the point of denying having opened any windows, Peter recognised the 'out' he needed. 'Um, yeah, I did have one open in the library last night. To cool it down, you know? I shut it this morning,' he went on, crossing mental fingers.

'Well, hopefully it's gone back out again, but nevertheless I think we'd better have a look around. We don't want it trapped in here making a mess.'

'Sure. Um… I just need to get my washing started and I'll come and help you.' He started rooting about in the washing machine, playing for time.

'Lost something?'

'Um, no… I forgot to check my pockets. There might be a biro…' Wasn't she ever going to take the hint? 'Why don't we split up and do different areas, that'll be faster.'

Mrs Butler gave him an odd look. 'In a hurry?'

'Just, you know… in case it *does* anything. We should find it before it, you know, pees on anything or that.' He pulled out a pair of jeans and started going through the pockets. They were empty, of course, but he drew it out as long as he could. He really didn't want to leave Binky alone in here without further direction and warnings not to touch anything. *Stay there!* he thought frantically at Binky. *Don't move, don't touch anything until I come back.* He had no idea if he was getting through or not. And then, with a cold crawling of horror up his spine, he remembered telling Binky to turn off the translator.

There was no help for it, and as he followed Mrs Butler up the corridor, as he numbly agreed to search the library and classrooms while she did the rest of the ground floor, he crossed his fingers as tightly as he could behind his back. With any luck, he thought, the kid might have one of his frequent naps.

Half an hour later, the ground floor having been searched assiduously on the one side by Mrs Butler and perfunctorily on the other by Peter, they met back in the main hall. Mrs Butler shook her head.

'Not a trace of anything. Did you find anything?'

'Nah. I reckon it must have already gone out the library window, when it was open.'

Mrs Butler sighed. 'I think we'd better check the other floors. You do the classrooms and the lab, and I'll check the staff quarters.'

He was half-heartedly peering under the desks in Room 2B (in case she came to check on him) when he heard it – a resounding bang from downstairs, followed by a faint hiss. It was the unmistakeable sound of the lid of a washing machine clanging into place, and the machine switching on, as they all did automatically once closed. He raced for the laundry, taking the stairs four at a time, praying that he'd get there first, and luck was on his side; Binky, having evidently knocked the lid, was sitting on the windowsill. He had just time to heave the window up, thanking God that it was an old-fashioned sash window, grab Binky and drop him out, before he heard the tapping of Mrs Butler's heels approaching down the passage.

He leaned out the window, gesturing at Binky to turn on the translator, and had only time for a single anguished command – HIDE – before she swept into the room.

'I heard a bang from in here, was that you, Peter?'

'It was the cat, it was in here the whole time, must have been behind the lid. I opened the window and chased it out.' He was babbling, he realised. Slow down, he admonished himself. Nothing looks more guilty than saying too much. He drew down the window and twisted the catch to lock it, keeping his back to her for a few seconds while he marshalled his thoughts.

'I heard that bang, and I rushed down here and there it was, so I opened up the window and shooed it out,' he repeated, surer of himself now as his story crystallised.

'That was quick thinking, Peter, well done.'

Quick thinking, thought Peter. You have absolutely no idea how quick.

That did it, Peter resolved on his way back up to collect his sheets. He had to find a way to activate the beacon somehow. They risked discovery every moment Binky was in the school. And what would happen when term started? He'd never be able to get to the attic then, and there certainly wasn't anywhere else Binky could safely hide.

It took them the rest of the afternoon to get all the washing through and dried. Peter occupied the time by telling Binky fairy tales. He was a gratifyingly receptive audience, only interrupting, on the average, every second sentence (What's a beard? What's a princess? What's a frog?) This gave the narratives a Wiki-esque quality that Peter rather enjoyed. He was discovering that there was a lot more to this big brother thing than worry and annoyance. There was a seductive quality about having someone hang on your every word and accept everything you said as gospel. He felt big, and wise, and reliable.

He left Binky curled on his bed while he went down to the cottage for dinner, examining a children's book he'd taken from the library, one with a lot of coloured pictures. He had a bowl of sardines and another of water, and Peter had extracted from him a solemn promise not to leave the room.

Dinner was a warm pork salad, enhanced with an Asian sauce. Peter made the whole thing himself under Mrs Butler's direction, while she sipped vodka. He had been rather suspicious at the idea of a warm salad, not to mention the combination of pork and plum sauce, but in the event the salad was delicious, and Mrs Butler promised to print him out a copy of it to keep. He would be able to amaze his parents next time he was home, she said. Peter didn't think he would be allowed in the embassy kitchens, but he was becoming quite fond of Mrs Butler, so he said nothing.

When he returned to his room, there was no sign of Binky. Full of foreboding, he climbed the stairs to the attic, where he found Binky emptying a box of old jewellery and sorting rings, necklaces and bracelets according to some unguessable criterion.

'Binky! What are you doing? You promised you'd stay in the room. You *promised!'*

<<Had to shit. My toilet's here.>> Binky seemed to feel this was a sufficient justification for breaking his solemn promise, and Peter, remembering how urgent such things could be when you were little, was inclined to agree.

<<I turned on the go home signal,>> Binky continued, his tone coming through the translator full of happy pride.

'What?' The bottom dropped out of Peter's stomach. He rushed to the pod and peered in. A small light was blinking above the white button. 'For God's sake, Binky. How do you know it isn't the self-destruct? What if it's going to blow up?'

Binky made that strange, sinuous movement that wasn't quite a shrug. <<Didn't blow up. Must be go home signal. Look, pretty!>> He held up a string of amethysts. <<Can I keep

it?>>

Peter mentally took back everything he'd said to himself that afternoon, about how great it was having a little kid around. The flashing light blinked on, either reassuring the beholder that help would soon be on the way or sending a cheerful message of doom. Would the school soon be replaced by a smoking crater?

'Binky, listen. How long does it take for the pod to blow up if you press the self – I mean the 'blow up' button?'

The shrug again. <<Don't know.>>

Peter felt his voice rising to a shriek, despite his effort at calm. 'Well, how do you know the button you pressed was the 'go home' one? How do you know it wasn't the 'blow up' one? Huh?'

<<Don't be cross. Look, you have this. Same as your eyes!>> He held out a bracelet, heavy with what looked like sapphires. Peter felt as if he'd kicked a

puppy. He ground his teeth and managed a smile.

'Thanks, Binky. I'll always keep it to remind me of you.' He shoved the bracelet into his pocket. It was only glass, he told himself. Real jewels wouldn't have been left in a mouldy old attic. 'Listen. How long does it take for the 'blow up' button to blow up the pod? It's important.'

<<Don't know. Told you. Anyway, it doesn't matter. Go home signal's going now. You can hear it.>>

'What d'you mean, I can hear it? I can't hear anything.'

<<Stupid! You listen!>> Binky tapped the translator box. <<Comes through this.>>

Peter closed his eyes and 'listened' as hard as he could, straining with his mind to pick up every bit of the translator's signal. Yes, now that he concentrated on the feed, he could detect something that hadn't been there before. A faint, faraway thread of need; a kind of calling. And superimposed somehow on it was some kind of identification; something that, somehow, meant 'Binky', just as clearly and absolutely as red meant stop.

☙CHAPTER TEN☙

Binky insisted on coming down to Peter's room to sleep. Peter argued a bit for form's sake, but he didn't really mind, even when Binky demanded a bedtime story, just like his little cousin, Fiona. Some things were the same no matter what planet you came from, he supposed. Probably most things. Kids were kids and stories were stories.

He told Binky Little Red Riding Hood (what's a wolf? what's a cloak? what's a cottage?) but this proved not to have been the best choice, for Binky was frightened by the wolf, and refused to let him turn out the light at nine o'clock. In vain did Peter explain about Lights Out. In vain did he point out that it was still light outside, and would be for at least another hour. The least movement towards the light switch resulted in a mental howling of anguish and fear. He resorted to another story, choosing The Frog Prince, on the basis that there was nothing scary in it. Unfortunately, however, Binky equated the well with his earlier experience falling into the washing machine, and yet a third story was required.

Third time lucky, thought Peter. He was running out of stories, and after the exciting day he'd had, he was running out of awake, too. The light really was starting to fade now, and he wanted to go to sleep. He devised a Cunning Plan.

'I'll tell you one more story,' he said, 'as long as we turn the light out, okay? Big boys sleep with the light off. It's only little babies that need it left on.'

This had the predicted effect, and Binky embraced the gathering dark with enthusiasm that was only partly feigned. Peter got back into bed and stretched out.

'Once upon a time,' he began, 'there were two children....'

He wondered if the witch in Hansel and Gretel would be too scary, but he drew out the beginning part, dwelling lengthily on the children's happy play and pleasant family life, and presently, while he was still embroidering on the theme of the family dog, the thread of awareness from the translator subsided into the dreamy, placid stream of Binky's sleeping mind.

They checked on the beacon in the morning, but it was winking away just as it had done before, and nothing seemed to have changed.

'How did you know which one it was?' Peter kept asking. It irritated him not to know; he couldn't quite believe that even the reckless Binky had merely shrugged and chosen one at random. Binky did not give any sensible answer; he seemed to be bored with the whole thing. <<Mum's coming soon,>> was all he would say. As to how he knew she was, he was silent, and Peter assumed it was nothing more than the blind faith that most small children have in the omnipotence of their mothers.

'How long will it take them to get here?' he tried, but this elicited only the shrug gesture. In the way of small children, Binky was confident that Mum was on the way, and the idea of quantifying seemed beyond him.

He didn't really enjoy his lunch, although it was fish and chips, which he loved, and Mrs Butler showed him how to coat the fish in a crisp batter and fry it in half an inch of oil, and how to make the chips in the oven after shaking them up in a bowl with a tiny smidgen of olive oil. He was constantly watching the window, waiting for a small green head to appear above the sill, and when he wasn't doing that he was worrying about all the trouble Binky could get himself into in the house. He had shepherded the child back to the attic and had ensured the door to the attic stairs was firmly closed, but he was by no means sure Binky couldn't open it with those clever, extendable fingers, and he was relieved beyond measure when the washing up was finished and he could go back to the main building.

As he was walking up the drive, he noticed a big, dark blue car turning in at the gate. He paused, wondering who would turn up in the middle of the Christmas holidays. Perhaps they were lost and wanted directions, but it seemed odd.

A tall man in a dark suit got out of the passenger side of the car and went to the gate. He appeared to be trying to open it. Peter sniggered. The gate was locked because the school was closed; Peter knew this, because when Mrs Butler had driven him into town, she had had to stop and unlock it, and lock it again after them. This, she had explained, was why it wasn't felt necessary to lock up the main building all the time; no one could get into the grounds.

The man was making a phone call now. He was waving his free arm a lot, and Peter thought he seemed angry. Presently he got back into the car, and it reversed out of the drive and went back the way it had come, back to the nearby township of Bondigong. Peter watched it fishtailing on the dirt road until it was out of sight. It gave him an uneasy feeling, but then of course he had never been at school during the holidays before. Perhaps they were health inspectors or something. By the time he reached the main building, his mind was fully occupied with Binky.

He found Binky in his room, chasing his tail. All the drawers were pulled out, and socks, t-shirts and underwear littered the floor. As he drew breath to shout about the mess, Binky caught sight of him, and paused in his circling. A wave of warmth and happiness and welcome washed over Peter, and he found he didn't have the heart to yell. He'd get Binky to help him pick everything up and put it away. He could make a game of it.

They had finished the t-shirts and were starting on the underwear when the door opened and Mrs Butler barged into the room. Don't knock or anything, Peter longed to say, but bit his tongue. Apart from anything else, he needed a minute to calm his breathing before speaking; Binky, primed with tales of wolves and wicked old witches, had dived under the bed as the door opened, whisking out of sight just in time.

'Peter! What on earth are you doing? Just look at this mess!'

'Um. Um. Well you see,' he improvised, 'I'm making my New Year's resolution this year to keep everything neat, and I thought it'd be easier if I sort of got started beforehand, so I'm rearranging my drawers, they were a bit messy.' *Can I weasel or what?* He wanted to punch the air as he saw her expression soften.

'Well, get that tidied away quick as you can. There are two gentlemen here from the government, they want a word with you.'

'Huh? What for?'

'Oh, some rubbish about a UFO sighting. They're interviewing everyone in the area, apparently. Honestly, the things they waste our money on. I put them in Mr Bamford's office. Don't be too long, alright? I'll be in my office.' She tap-tapped away. Peter listened to her diminishing footsteps until they reached the end of the corridor. Why hadn't he heard her approaching? He had to be more careful.

Of more immediate concern, however, were these 'government men', whoever they were. Brought up from an early age to distrust strangers, Peter wasn't sure he could rely on Mrs Butler to check their credentials. He'd ask to see their I.D. first thing, he decided. They might be terrorists, intent on kidnapping an ambassador's son.

Binky was curled into a shivering ball under

the bed, his tail wrapped over his face. He had switched off his translator, Peter supposed because he'd told him to turn it off the other time, in the laundry. You couldn't fault the kid for learning. Smart as a whip, he was. Peter had to poke him three times before he would look up. He gestured at the translator box, and Binky turned it on, unleashing a howling wave of fear that turned Peter's bowels to water. He made frantic lowering motions, pushing down the air with his hands, until Binky got the message and lowered the intensity; it was like a volume control, regulating how strongly one received its messages.

'Listen. There's two men from the government downstairs. They want to talk to me. Don't *move* from here until I get back, okay? And better turn that off again. I think they're looking for you. Mrs B said a UFO sighting, that must have been the pod.' He rested his hand for a moment on Binky's back, trying to still the terrified quaking. Poor little guy.

He found the two men in Farty McBumface's office. As he entered the room, not knocking since McBumface wasn't there, he saw one of them straighten up behind the desk. He'd been snooping in Farty's drawers, Peter was sure. Mrs Butler was nowhere to be seen.

'Where's Mrs Butler?'

'Ah, now you must be Peter.' The man moved out from behind the desk, dripping geniality like a dentist with a needle behind his back. Peter could feel his fur standing on end. Why did adults think that fake nicey-nice business was at all attractive or convincing?

'Have a seat, Peter, that's right. I'm Mr Kane.' Peter sat on the edge of the visitor's chair. Instead of going behind the desk and sitting in Mr Bamford's chair, the man sat on the front edge of the desk, swinging one leg in a way that Peter supposed was meant to look casual.

'So, what have you been doing with

yourself, all alone here in the holidays? Parents let you down, eh?' He didn't wait for an answer. 'You need to answer a few questions, then you can go.'

Peter's back was well and truly up now. Holidays with his diplomatic parents had attuned him, more than most children his age, to the nuances of language, and the 'you need to' offended him.

'Now, did you see anything unusual in the last week?'

'Yes, sir.' Peter couldn't resist winding him up. He arranged his features into his best 'eager helpfulness' expression.

Kane had stiffened. He telegraphed everything, Peter thought disdainfully.

'And what was that? Something in the sky, perhaps?'

'Oh, no, sir, right here in this room.'

Blank astonishment replaced the sharp keenness on the man's face.

'What, in here?'

'Yes, sir.'

'What was it?'

'You, sir.'

'What – I'm not unusual.'

'Well, sir, I've never seen you before. And it's unusual, isn't it, to be going about asking questions at a closed school? I mean, normally there wouldn't be anyone here to ask.'

Kane sighed. Peter could see him decide that he, Peter, was retarded. It might as well have been written across his forehead in big, red letters.

'Peter, my colleague and I are from the government. We're investigating reports of an unidentified flying object in this area, and certain signals which appear to be emanating from this site. In the interests of National Security,' – his tone supplied the capital letters – 'you need to tell us everything you know, right now. Understand?'

'Everything, sir?'

'Ab-so-lutely everything. There are consequences for obstructing us, do you understand that? This is not the bloody X-files you're dealing with, son. This is Border Force. We have certain... powers to enforce compliance.'

'I don't know what you mean, sir.' Inwardly, Peter was quaking. He had never encountered such hostility from an adult before. Adults in Peter's experience were either vaguely kind, impersonally authoritarian, or completely uninterested in him. They weren't, somehow, real in the way that other kids were real. But this man and his colleague, somehow, were frighteningly real. Where was the other bloke, anyway? Peter started to turn to look behind him, but his shirt front was gripped, lifting him half out of his chair. Kane's face was thrust into his own. A tiny part of Peter's mind registered that he could feel the man's breath on his face. He squirmed, trying to break free.

'You will co-operate with us,' Kane ground out, '*one way or another*. And I really don't care which. Do you understand me?' He gave Peter a little shake and thrust him roughly back into the chair, then looked up, past Peter, and gave a little nod. Behind him, unpleasantly close behind him, he heard a flicking sound, and smelt smoke. The second man moved into view. He had lit a cigarette, and was smiling in a way that, somehow, Peter didn't like. He had a very bad feeling about this.

'Um, there's no smoking on the school gr–'

'The end of a cigarette burns at more than five hundred degrees Centigrade, did you know that, Peter?'

The other man took a deep drag of the cigarette, sucking down the smoke with relish. He tapped ash onto the floor, then leaned forward and blew a jet of smoke into Peter's face. Peter started to cough, his stomach heaving at the smell of it. He leaned away from the cloud, but Kane had gripped his shirt again and held him in place.

'Now, can you imagine what that does to your skin, if you should, accidentally of course, happen to come in contact with the burning end?'

☙CHAPTER ELEVEN☙

Peter's mind whirled, round and round in tiny circles of panic.

'I don't know anything, sir, really I don't.'

'Don't bullshit me, you little snot. We've triangulated that signal right to this building, you get that? Now, either you–'

SLAM! Peter jumped as behind him, the door crashed open. Kane stood up, releasing his shirt, and both men stepped back and straightened.

'WHAT is going on here?'

Turning, Peter hardly recognised Mrs Butler. She seemed, somehow, to have puffed herself up like a blowfish. On one level he saw the thirtyish blonde woman with stretch jeans and high heels and brightly-painted fingernails. On another level, it was as if Attila the Hun stood there, backed by a fierce horde.

'We're just –'

'Just WHAT? Just INTERROGATING A CHILD WITHOUT AN ADULT PRESENT? Peter,' she added in a more normal tone, 'go to your room. I'll talk to you in a minute. Go on, off you go. Right now.'

His breath coming fast, Peter left his chair and sprinted for the door, expecting every moment to be called back. He made it to the door and slipped out, pulling it closed behind him, but even in his panic, curiosity won out and he didn't quite close it, nor did he go to his room as bidden, although he crouched ready to run if the strangely fierce Mrs Butler took a step in his direction.

Mrs Butler was no longer shouting, and Peter strained to hear what was being said. The heavy door, even a little bit open, blocked most sound and the Head's desk was at the other end of the vast room, the better to intimidate pupils who had to walk the vast expanse of carpet from the door. He caught the words 'taking advantage', and a low murmur from one of the men; he couldn't be sure which, but assumed it was Kane, who had seemed to be in charge.

'OH, REALLY?' The blast of authority in her tone rocked Peter back on his heels, and he almost fell over. 'NOT WITHOUT A WARRANT, BUSTER.'

Another murmur, fainter than before. The daunting Kane sounded almost cowed. Peter didn't blame him; despite the terror the man had inspired in him only moments before, he felt almost sorry for him. He was discovering a new respect for Mrs Butler.

The voices rose and fell, but Peter detected a definite valedictory tone creeping into the exchange. Time to make tracks before he was discovered. Listening at doors was one of the most despised behaviours at Tarrington; it was *sneaky*, and no one liked a sneak. His ears burned just thinking about getting caught at it.

He regained his room, panting, and had just time to check on Binky, who seemed to have fallen asleep, calm his breathing and arrange himself on the bed in a carefree posture with *Watership Down*, which he still had not finished reading. He left his shoes on, in the hope that Mrs Butler would focus on the rule infraction, and would therefore not pay much attention to anything else in the room.

Presently he heard her tap-tap-tapping along the corridor. Unusually, she also tapped on his door before putting her head round it. She advanced into the room and sat, most uncharacteristically, on the end of his bed, paying no attention to the illegal shoes other than to make a tutting sound and shove his feet off the bed.

'Peter,' she began, 'I'm sorry you had to be subjected to that.'

'It's okay, Mrs Butler,' said Peter. It wasn't okay, it was very far from okay, but he didn't want to look like a whiny little kid, and he didn't want to prolong Mrs Butler's presence in his room, either, in case Binky woke up. 'I won't have to see them again, will I?'

Mrs Butler compressed her lips. 'I wish I could promise you that, but I'm afraid you may have to. But not on your own, Peter. I'll be there if you have to talk to them again. You should have come and got me just now, I thought you understood. Minors have to have an adult present if they're questioned by the police, it's the law. Never forget that. If they try to talk to you on your own, just tell them I forbid it.'

'But they've gone now, haven't they? Are they coming back?'

Mrs Butler sighed. 'They want to search the house and grounds. I sent them packing, but they say they'll be back with a warrant, and if they get one there'll be nothing I can do. I can insist on being present during the search, but that's all. I've already rung up Mr Bamford, and he's coming back as soon as he can manage it. In the meantime, just stay out of their way if they come back. I'd advise you to stay in your room as much as possible, or if you'd rather, you can come down to the cottage.'

'I think I'd rather stay here, if that's alright,' said Peter. 'I've still got a lot of the holiday reading list Mr Bamford gave me.'

'Alright, then. But anything bothers you, Peter, anything at all mind, you come straight down to the cottage, okay?'

'Will do, Mrs Butler.'

She got up from the bed and went to the door. 'Oh, and Peter,' she said as she opened it. 'You'll get on better with that book if you turn it the right way up.'

They were coming back. They were coming back. The phrase reverberated in his mind with the urgency of a drumbeat summoning him to war. It was Binky they were after; somehow, somewhere, someone had picked up the signal from the beacon and they'd followed it here. And it was the government, or the police or the army, or perhaps all three. He quailed at the thought of massive, powerful forces mustering unseen against him. For it was against him, he realised; there was no one else. And he was just one small, skinny twelve-year-old. He knew, in his deepest mind, that it was ridiculous even to think of standing against the might of the government, with all their adults, their guns, their military tracking equipment. And yet, there was Binky, just a little kid, and lost. They wouldn't get Binky, he vowed. Not as long as there was anything he could do to stop them.

Well, he thought, tucking Binky, who had at some point in his cogitations crawled out from under the bed and nestled against him, into his elbow, they had their radars and their agents and all the rest of it. What did he have? There was the pod, with whatever technology it held. That was both asset and liability, since it was presumably, along with Binky, the target of the threatened search. It had its camouflage, he remembered. It had looked like an ordinary cardboard box to him until he had gone right up to it. Binky, though, Binky had no camouflage.

One thing he did have on his side, Peter thought, was an intimate knowledge of the building, which they lacked. If he shoved the bookcase back up against the door to the attic stairs, might they overlook it, as generations of boys had done? It was worth a try. That would keep them from finding the pod. Should he leave Binky, also, back in the attic? But the thought of leaving the child alone and frightened displeased him. If only there were some way of camouflaging Binky himself.

And then he remembered his first, tentative

explorations of the house. It seemed like years ago, back before he'd met Binky, but hadn't there been something – yes, he remembered; it was Mr Bamford's bottle of Raven Oil, in his bathroom cabinet. He remembered, with the nostalgia of age for callow youth, his excitement at the thought that *Farty McBumface dyed his hair and he, Peter, was the only one who knew it.*

Mrs Butler had to have reached the cottage by now, so the coast ought to be clear. Nevertheless, Peter's heart pounded as he crept down the two flights of stairs and along the passage to her office. The keys were hanging by the door, and he snatched them from their hook, running back up the stairs, heart pounding as he unlocked Bamford's door and raced for the bathroom, and grabbed the little bottle. There was a packet of cotton wool and he took that too; he would need something to apply the stuff with. Quickly he closed the cabinet and retreated, leaving everything as before. Another sprint down to replace the keys. He was both panting and sweaty when he regained the dubious sanctuary of his room.

'Binky,' he began, gesturing to Binky to turn the translator back on, 'listen. We're going to have to disguise you.'

<<What's disguise? Have the bad people gone away?>>

'They've gone for now, but they might come back, and we need to make you look like someone else, alright? So that if they see you, they won't notice you.'

<<Why?>>

'Well, because you'll look like a cat.'

<<What's a cat?>>

'It's a kind of animal. And you look a bit like one, well from a distance anyway, if you were black. So we're going to make you black.'

<<Why?>>

'Because then they won't – oh, sod it. Just

because, alright?' That was the other thing about little kids, Peter remembered. The interminable questions, and once they got on a run of 'why?' you couldn't get them off it to save your life. 'Look,' he went on, 'time is of the essence.' He'd heard the phrase on television, and loved the important sound of it. 'Now, keep still, alright? I'm going to put this on you.'

<<What is it? Can I taste it?>>

'No, it's poisonous.' Peter had no idea whether Raven Oil was actually poisonous, but it did say 'Not To Be Taken'. Also, he realised, he had no idea whether Binky's outward similarity to a cat meant he might lick his fur. Better safe than sorry. 'You have to be very careful never to get this in your mouth, okay?' He unscrewed the cap, wishing the bottle were larger. Hopefully, a little would go a long way. He tipped a careful amount onto a wad of cotton wool and applied it to Binky's back, spreading it down his side. Binky instantly craned his neck around to sniff at it.

<<YUK! NASTY!>>

'Alright, just hold still, the smell goes away once it gets dry.' He hoped.

<<NASTY! DO NOT WANT! GET IT OFF GET IT OFF!>>

'Look, keep still, will you? You'll–'

But it was too late; Binky had leaped onto the bed and was shaking himself like a dog. Droplets of Raven Oil flew about, decorating wall, pillow and blankets with tiny black spots. Peter set the bottle out of the way on his desk.

'Binky, come on, this is going to stop the bad men from catching you.'

<<NASTY! DO NOT WANT! WANT MY MUM!>>

'Your mum wants you to have this stuff on,' lied Peter. The barrage of misery that had been buffeting his mind eased a little.

<<No, she doesn't.>>

'Yes, she does.' It was true in a way, Peter told himself. He was sure Binky's mum wanted him to be safe. 'And she wants you to hurry, because we don't know when those government guys are coming back. And,' he added, desperate to get off the subject of Binky's mum before Binky questioned how he knew what she wanted, 'if you keep still and let me do this, I'll give you a whole tin of sardines.'

<<SARDINES YAY! Let's go and get them now.>>

'After the black stuff,' said Peter firmly.

৪০CHAPTER TWELVE৩

The result was a bit patchy, but as long as you didn't look at him too closely, Peter thought Binky could pass for a rather skinny black cat. From a distance. The plan was that they would keep watch on the driveway, and as soon as any car appeared, they would immediately run downstairs, where Peter would let Binky out the side door. Binky would take cover under some bushes, emerging only when he heard Peter give a certain complicated whistle. They had practised the drill three times, and Peter thought it would be alright, providing they didn't come after dark, when they might conceivably get up to the house undetected. Accordingly, he positioned himself on the window seat on the second floor landing, which commanded a view of the drive all the way down to the cottage. They'd have to stop at the cottage, wouldn't they, to show the warrant to Mrs Butler, if they got one?

In the event, it was not until the following afternoon that the car appeared. They had spent a tense and irritable evening watching the driveway. Peter had tried to teach Binky to play 'I spy', but it had not been a success, as the whole thing depended on spelling, and his efforts to adapt it by replacing the initial letter with a different sort of clue had, ultimately, failed. Binky wasn't sophisticated enough to grasp the concept, it seemed. Or perhaps it was too alien for him. Perhaps they didn't have guessing games where he came from. He'd tried 'Animal, vegetable or mineral', but there again they had foundered on the rock either of cultural differences or of Binky's youth. The telepathic translator could only go so far, he was finding. By the time the car appeared, Peter had been grinding his teeth with frustration and annoyance. Binky had fared better, curling up for brief naps every couple of hours, but Peter didn't dare trust him to keep watch for more than the few minutes it took him to dash to the bathroom. His childish mind was too easily distracted, so Peter's only relief from his vigil had been the rushed and sweaty half hour he'd taken to move all the books and shove the bookcase at the foot of the attic stairs back flush against the wall, during which time he'd sent Binky out the side door to practise hiding under bushes.

As expected, the car drew to a halt outside the gates, and before long Mrs Butler emerged from the cottage and marched down the driveway. Peter couldn't see her face, but from the way she was moving, he thought she looked as if she were furious. She opened the gate and went out, and two men, whom Peter couldn't identify at that distance but who he assumed were Kane and his associate, got out of the car. They stood together, the men hulking just that little bit too close in a way that reminded him of a couple of bullies monstering a little kid, although he found it hard to imagine anyone bullying Mrs Butler. He couldn't make out much at that distance, but it looked like one of them was showing her something, some papers. Presently all three of them got into the car, Mrs Butler in the front, and it started slowly up the drive.

It was lucky they'd practised, Peter thought as he pelted back to the staircase from the side door. The car took less time than he'd expected to come up the drive, and they only made it by a whisker. As the front door opened, he had just enough time to about-face and pretend he was going the other way. Lucky they'd used the side door and not the one at the back, which opened from the kitchen passage; the library was in this direction.

Mrs Butler was first through the door, spotting Peter and running to him. She bent close to him and whispered in a rush, as Kane barged through the door, yelling into his mobile phone.

'Get up to your room and pack what you need for overnight. You're coming down to the cottage until they've gone; I don't like the look of these people, and I don't want you anywhere near them, understood? Hurry, now. I'll be up in a minute.' She straightened as Kane approached, blocking his way as Peter raced up the stairs. Outside, he heard gravel scatter as another vehicle drew up; it sounded like they'd slammed on the brakes in a hurry, and he prayed Binky wasn't doing anything silly.

As he shoved pyjamas, washbag and a change of clothes into his backpack, he could hear the tramping of many feet below; shouted commands and the crackling of some kind of radio gave the affair a military kind of sound. He finished his meagre packing, and sat down on his bed to wait for

Mrs Butler. Her advice to avoid the men seemed very sound to him; there was something about the commotion downstairs that conveyed a feeling of hostility, of enemy forces. Were these people really from the government, he wondered. But then, he supposed they must have been legitimate, or they wouldn't have been able to get the warrant. For the first time, he wondered if the court was really on his side, or rather, the side of the good guys. He'd been brought up to take for granted that the police were there to protect everyone, that the army, on a larger scale, was there for the same reason. But the memory of Kane's cold, amoral eyes as he mused about cigarette burns stuck in his throat like a bitter pill. It wasn't only Binky who was in danger.

His worry about Binky paced up and down, a leopard in the cage of his mind. He dared not sneak down to check on him; any movement might draw the attention of the searchers. To take his mind off the worry, he moved about the room, tidying and straightening. No sense getting on Mrs B's wrong side, especially if he was going to be cooped up with her for who knew how long. He added *Watership Down* and his reading list to the backpack, guiltily aware of how little reading he had done since the start of the holiday. He was still only a quarter of the way through the first book.

As he pushed the book into his backpack, the mess on his dresser caught his eye, the little bottle of Raven Oil, flanked by damp wads of blackened cotton wool. He added those to the backpack, too, in an outer pocket so as not to stain his clothes; he'd flush the cotton wool away down the toilet, first chance he got. He wouldn't risk it here. In fact, he decided, he wouldn't so much as poke his nose outside his door until Mrs Butler got there. There were times when doing as you were told really was the wisest and safest course.

He experienced a rush of nostalgia for the time before the holidays had started, when his biggest conflict with authority had been pulling up the bedspread to hide the fact he hadn't made his bed properly, or not doing all of his assigned homework. That feeling of rightness before the world, of safety, which he had never really noticed but which had, he now realised, formed part of the fabric of his whole life up till now, was gone, vanished as if it had never been, and he mourned its loss as if it had been a dead child. The utter loneliness of his position struck him with such force that he recoiled as if from a physical blow. He could not now recall the frame of mind that had filled him with such exultation to know something that no one else in the world knew. Such knowledge was more to be feared than cherished, he now felt. It cut like a knife, severing him from everything he had held dear, taking his very safety in question and leaving him starkly alone, and, he now knew, hunted. Because that was what they were doing, wasn't it, those men downstairs with their tromping boots and harsh cries and, he had no doubt, their guns? They were hunting Binky, and by extension, they were hunting him, the one who had sheltered Binky. The knowledge blew through his mind like a cold wind, and he shivered.

Mrs Butler found him like that, hunched over, clutching his stomach.

'Peter, what's the matter? Do you feel sick? You're as white as a sheet.' She laid a hand on his forehead, checking for fever and shaking her head. 'Come along out of this now; we'll go straight down the stairs and out the door, okay? If anyone speaks to you, just look straight ahead and leave me to do the talking.' She picked up his backpack and took his arm. 'Come on, now. It's almost over, and we'll have you down to the cottage in two shakes of a lamb's tail.'

The homely expression almost surprised Peter into tears. He pressed his knuckle firmly against his top lip, a technique Aunty Jean had taught him for driving back the urge to cry. It worked, unlike many of those old wives' things. He took a deep breath, relieved to find it steady.

There were armed men stationed at the front door, two on each side, with what looked to Peter's inexperienced eye like machine guns. He had been right, then, to guess at military involvement; they wore camouflage, and were therefore soldiers. Peter wished he could decipher the stripes on their sleeves, but as the only contact he'd ever had with military people had been at various foreign embassies, he knew only the ranks from major up.

More than anything else, the baked beans on toast Mrs Butler produced for dinner convinced Peter his fears were real. They settled to watch the evening news, but he noticed she selected the channel with the local news instead of the ABC national news. Oddly, there was no mention of anything about a UFO sighting.

'Mrs Butler?'

'Yes, Peter?'

'How come there's nothing on the news about it?'

Mrs Butler stared straight ahead, her face set into hard lines. 'I don't know, Peter, but it's not a good sign, not good at all. Look, I think I ought to phone your parents. What time is it going to be now, in Carthania?'

'I dunno. About lunchtime, I think.'

'Alright, well I think I'd better let them know what's going on. They're in the Diplomatic Service, aren't they?'

'Yes, well Dad is. He's the Ambassador.'

'I don't suppose you have the number for the embassy there?'

Peter was about to reply when several gunshots sounded from up the hill. They both froze.

'Right, I've had enough of this. I'm going up there to speak to their C.O. Peter, you stay here, alright? Lock the door after me and don't let anyone in, no matter what.' She was moving around the room as she spoke, closing the windows and drawing the curtains. 'No matter what, do you understand? Just sit tight until I get back.'

Peter was in agony. He felt like a coward, leaving Binky out there on his own, being shot at, but he didn't know what he could do, either. The disguise plan was, he knew, full of holes; Binky would not pass for a cat if seen up close, no matter what; the translator box hung around his neck would ensure that, even if nothing else did. Perhaps they'd already killed him.

If he tried to go up there now, he would be exposed on that long, bare driveway; Mrs Butler would be sure to see him coming behind her.

He was still agonising when he heard the door, and Mrs Butler stomped into the room, muttering. She marched straight to the drinks cabinet and poured herself a stiff vodka.

'Those bloody morons. Shooting at a cat, apparently. I've spoken to their officer. Bloody morons.'

Peter's blood turned to ice water. 'Shooting at a cat? What for? They didn't hit it, did they?'

Mrs Butler seemed to become aware of him all at once. 'Hit it? I doubt if those idiots could hit the side of a barn.'

'But it's important,' he wanted to say. 'I have to know.' The words died on his lips. No animals were kept at the school, so if there had been a cat, it would have been a stray, and while it was reasonable to express concern, it would be suspicious to go too far with it.

'It must be a stray,' he ventured. 'That cat that was in the laundry must have been it. We should put out food and water for it.'

Mrs Butler looked mistily at him. 'You're a good boy, Peter. Of course we must take care of it. But right now, I don't want you going anywhere near that lot. Once this stupid business is over, we'll find it and do something, I promise. Right, now. Your parents.'

But when she picked up the receiver, there was an odd little silence, and she set the receiver gently in its cradle without dialling.

'The phone's out.'

&CHAPTER THIRTEEN&

They sat in silence for a moment, digesting this.

'What if they've cut it,' suggested Peter.

'Don't be silly, Peter, that sort of thing's only in the movies. These people are the Australian army, after all. They don't go round cutting people's telephone lines. We've nothing to fear from them.'

Why did you tell me not to let anyone in, then, Peter wanted to ask. He didn't, though.

Something told him he wouldn't like the answer, and that it would be unkind. More to the point was, what was he going to do about Binky? It was now almost eight o'clock, and Binky had been outside by himself for more than six hours, with no food and no-one to keep him out of trouble. If they hadn't already shot him, he reminded himself bitterly.

He was going to have to sneak out, he decided. He'd wait until full dark, and go out the window. The cottage's spare room window looked toward the road, so he would be hidden from the main house while he climbed out, and it wasn't that much of a drop. Getting back in might be a bit more of a problem, but he'd worry about that when he came to it.

Mrs Butler had been fiddling with her mobile and shaking her head. 'I can't get any signal. It's weird; usually I get three bars here. I'll try upstairs.' She disappeared up the narrow stairs, but was back before Peter had time to do more than start a mental list of stuff he needed to pinch from her kitchen to feed Binky.

'There's no signal at all. There must be a problem.'

'Yeah,' said Peter. 'There's a problem alright. Soldiers all over the school, letting off guns and carrying on.'

Mrs Butler paused in the act of sitting down, and remained frozen in an odd and undignified crouch for several seconds.

'You know, Peter, I think you're right. Get your things. We're going into town.'

'What – get my stuff, you don't mean we're going to stay in there?'

'That's exactly what I mean. Mr Bamford said he was on his way, but I don't know how long it will take him to get here – his wife isn't well, you know, and I spoke to him before – well, I think we're better out of it at the moment. We'll call in at the police station and sort this out, and then I think we'll stay at the pub tonight.'

The words were out before he could stop them. 'But I can't leave Binky!'

He was mentally kicking himself even before he finished speaking, but even as inside, he wailed in despair and clutched at the words to call them back, Mrs Butler was misting up.

'Oh, you poor little mite. I forgot how young you were. Well, Binky will just have to get on without you for one night. Now come on – get your things together. It's almost eight already.'

She was up the stairs and back, holding in one hand a small bag and in the other Peter's backpack, before he could think what to do. As they rolled down the drive in the evening light, he craned his neck, scanning the bushes around the school building for a hint of movement, for a small, black body, but all he saw were a couple of camouflage-clad men pacing back and forth on the forecourt.

'You're going to break your neck, Peter, if you're not careful,' said Mrs Butler, crunching to a halt in front of the big iron gates. 'I don't remember closing the gates. Those silly soldiers obviously aren't country boys.'

'Country boys?' Peter couldn't see the connection.

'Yes, in the country, you know, you must always leave gates exactly as you found them – open, shut, halfway, whatever. Unless they're your own gates, of course. It's very bad manners not to.'

Peter tucked this nugget of information into the back of his mind and was about to turn around for another desperate attempt to spot Binky when three soldiers stepped into view from behind the big elm tree. One approached the car, while the other two took up a position in front of the gate, and they were – well, they weren't quite *pointing* them at the car, but they *were* holding guns, big ones, and they were holding them in the *direction* of the car.

'Sorry, ma'am,' said the third soldier,

bending to the window. 'I'm afraid you can't leave.'

'What the hell do you mean, I can't leave? Get your men out of the way right now.'

'I'm sorry, ma'am. No-one in or out, those are my orders. You'll have to take it up with Captain Gregory.'

'Now you see here. I am going into town, I am taking this child somewhere safe, where there aren't *idiots* letting off *firearms*, and you are going to get the *hell* out of my way, am I making myself clear?'

Peter had never seen Mrs Butler in such a bate, even that time he and Jenkins Minor had started the food fight, back in Remove. He felt quite sorry for the soldier. Nevertheless, instead of quailing before her wrath, the man simply shook his head and glanced at the two men in front of the gate, and they were – yes, they *were – lifting their rifles until they pointed straight at the car.* It was unreal somehow, like a nightmare, Peter thought even as a cold clutch of fear gripped his stomach, the kind of nightmare where some innocuous object in your daily life suddenly grew teeth and bit you.

Mrs Butler had rolled up the window and was turning the car around. As they headed back up the drive, he could see the soldiers, still pointing their rifles *right at the car*.

At least, he comforted himself as he got ready for bed, he hadn't had to leave the school and abandon Binky. He laid his clothes in reverse order on top of his backpack, ready to be found in the dark. He opened the window as high as it would go. The cottage was stifling; Mrs Butler had closed and locked all the downstairs windows, and had shoved an armchair in front of the door, as if she expected an attack.

He'd managed to filch two cans of sardines from the kitchen while she was in the bathroom, but water was going to be a problem. There were various taps dotted about the grounds, but they needed to get out of the school grounds and into the state forest, the outskirts of which nestled enticingly against the six-foot fence at the bottom of the lower playing fields. He'd need a bottle of some kind, preferably already filled. If only Mrs Butler had been a water snob, like his mother, there'd have been bottles of spring water in the pantry.

Mrs Butler did have one thing in common with his mother, though. They both liked vodka. Even better, Mrs Butler, unlike his mother, poured her own, from a bottle that sat on top of that drinks cabinet in the corner of the sitting room. Just half an hour ago he'd watched her pour herself a drink. The bottle had a screw top.

That was the plan, then. He'd creep downstairs once she was asleep, grab the bottle and fill it up with water. He'd have to tip out the rest of the vodka, but Peter thought that was all to the good – it always made his mother bad-tempered, although it didn't seem to have much effect on Mrs

Butler.

He switched out the light and got into bed, sitting up so he wouldn't fall asleep. He could hear Mrs Butler moving around in her room across the hall, and then the faint creak of bedsprings. An eternity followed, during which Peter stared at the faint light that emanated from under her door. He could hear the occasional rustle of a page turning. He hoped it was a boring book. *You are getting sleepy,* he chanted in his mind. *Your eyelids are growing heavy...* no, that wouldn't do – he was starting to get sleepy himself! He'd count the seconds between page turns. If the time got longer, that would show she was getting tired.

It seemed like a hundred years before he heard the window open and saw the light blink off. He counted to a thousand before he dared move.

Upstairs there had been a little light from the sky, but downstairs, with every window shut and every curtain drawn, it was pitch black;

he almost felt his face to make sure his eyes were really open. Inch by careful inch he shuffled across the floor, hands outstretched in front of him, bare feet sliding along the carpet. The drinks cabinet was a bit to the left of where he'd expected to find it, and he almost came to grief then as his groping hand knocked the bottle, but he managed to grab it before it went over and stood clutching it, quaking in the dark, breathing in through the nose and out through the mouth, as he had once read would overcome fear. Then he retraced his path, feeling with his toes before every step until he could grasp the stair rail.

The bathroom door safely locked behind him, he debated for a moment whether to turn on the light, but the risk of knocking something off and making a noise in the unfamiliar room decided him. There was, after all, nothing odd about going to the lavatory. He poured the vodka down the basin drain and rinsed the bottle six times, blessing his decision to turn on the light as he realised he could not fit it under the basin tap, and must use the one in the bath.

The bottle finally as clean as he could get it, he filled it with cold water and wiped off the outside on the towel he'd used earlier. He spent five minutes listening before he opened the door, and heard nothing, but just in case she was awake, he flushed the lavatory and briefly ran the tap again before switching off the light and opening the door, the bottle prudently concealed under his pyjama top.

Once in the safety of his bedroom, he closed the door as quietly as he could manage before embarking on his final preparations. Inch by stealthy inch he drew on his clothes.

The bottle chinked against the sardine cans in the backpack, so he wrapped his pyjamas around it. Then he crept to the window and leaned far out. It appeared to be a sheer drop down to the rose bushes that bordered the cottage. Peter cursed himself for not checking that out before, although he didn't know what he could have done about it. He didn't fancy landing on top of one of those bushes. He'd have to jump as far out as he could manage, and hope to miss them and land on the grass. For a moment he quailed, but then he thought of Binky, alone, hungry, cold and frightened, and without giving himself time for second thoughts he tossed the backpack out to one side and climbed onto the windowsill.

Viewed from this angle, the ground looked a lot farther down than he'd expected. He'd planned to hang from the sill by his hands and drop, which would have made it, he thought, only about ten feet, a safe enough distance. Now, however, he was going to have to jump from the sill. What if he landed badly and hurt his ankle?

Drop and roll, that was the thing, like they'd done in gym class. He took a deep breath, let it out, took another, shut his eyes tightly and jumped.

☙CHAPTER FOURTEEN☙

He had an instant to regret the childish impulse that had led him to shut his eyes before the ground slammed into him, and it turned out that dropping and rolling was not a matter of choice after all. Breathing didn't seem to be an available choice either, and he started to panic until he realised he'd landed on his back, and had winded himself, that was all, come on, you know how to deal with this, it happened before in a football game…. The voice of Mr Woodrow came back to him: *relax, it doesn't last, stay calm, crouch over, that's right, and take a slow, slow breath, gently and slowly, see, you can get some air in, it's like a seatbelt, it only stops you if you're too sudden, as long as you're gentle you can pull it right out, and you can breathe too, as long as you stay calm…*

'Thanks, Mr Woodrow,' muttered Peter. He was breathing easily now, and he sat up and looked about for his backpack. He found it some way to the left of where he'd expected it to be, and his luck was still running; the precious bottle of water hadn't broken.

There was no light from the cottage, so it looked as if he'd got away clean, without waking Mrs Butler. He had, he reckoned, until at least seven o'clock before she noticed his absence.

In that time he had somehow to find Binky, in a military camp full of armed and hostile soldiers, get him away without getting caught, and get somewhere safe. And then, somehow survive until Binky's parents came for him. After that, he supposed it didn't matter, he could just come back; he'd be in a lot of trouble, but that was life as a kid, you were always in trouble for something or other. He could say he'd been frightened of the soldiers or something. It was lucky, really, that the government guy had been so horrible. He'd make that his excuse.

But where to go, how to keep Binky safe, and all this without knowing how long they would need to keep hidden, that loomed over him like a vast, dark burden, and he was crushed by it.

'It's not fair,' he wanted to howl. 'I'm only twelve.'

But there it was, and there was Binky, and Binky was only six, or whatever the alien equivalent was. Sighing, he dragged on the backpack, with its weight of adult responsibilities, and set off up the hill, avoiding the long, bare driveway, crouching over and making little darts from one tree to the next.

The moon was fully up now, and in its light Peter could see, from his position behind the gardener's shed, lights in a number of the downstairs rooms, although the upper stories were dark. By luck or good management (probably luck, he told himself) he had made it all the way around to the back of the building without being seen. The problem was, what to do now? Anything he did to attract Binky's attention would also attract the attention of the little cluster of soldiers who stood around the back door smoking, in defiance of the school's Smoke-Free Environment policy.

If only he hadn't made Binky turn off the telepathic translator. A wave of hopelessness swelled and broke in his mind. He was all alone, it was way past his bedtime, and he was cold, and he had no idea, absolutely none, what to do next. He'd get caught, he was probably guilty of ninety-seven Federal crimes, and Mrs Butler would never believe he hadn't drunk the vodka. He'd be expelled for that, if nothing else.

He wasn't going to blubber like a little kid, though, not him. It was the cold making his nose run and his eyes water. He had to come up with a plan. He curled himself into a ball, his mind a blank.

He never knew how long it was before a persistent, sharp poking at his shoulder recalled him to himself. At first he thought it was some sharp projection on the wall of the shed, and shifted irritably away, but the poking continued, and whatever was doing it was so obviously moving that he opened his eyes, and impossibly, there was Binky, ratty and dishevelled, but very much alive.

He had snatched Binky up before he thought, in a hug of utter relief. Binky let out a squeak of protest and wriggled violently. Peter froze, loosening his grip but not otherwise moving. Voices drifted to him from the back door.

'What was that? You hear something?'

'Nah.'

'Like a squeak.'

'Prob'ly a rat.'

'Got the big torch?'

Peter froze, holding his breath, as footsteps crunched towards the garden shed. Could Binky get to cover? But there was no way to communicate with him with the translator off. He could see the torch beam sweeping back and forth across the yard. Blood pounded in his ears, and he felt his insides go soft with terror. Just as he was about to break and run for it, in a last frantic attempt at escape that he knew in advance was doomed to failure, a voice rang out.

'You men! What d'you think you're doing?'

'Jenks heard a rat, Sarge.'

'Get back on the job. I'll give you rats. No more smoke breaks until you've finished searching the second floor.'

The torch beam cut off abruptly, and the approaching footsteps receded again, at a considerably smarter pace. Presently, the slam of a door could be heard, and when, after a few minutes, Peter ventured a look around the corner of the shed, the door was closed, and no one was in sight.

Ignoring Binky's frantic wriggling, Peter rose to a half-crouch and ran for his life. Once they'd passed the tennis courts, the land fell away in a long, even slope towards the lower playing fields, and they were out of sight of the main house, at least he hoped they were. If he couldn't see the house, he reasoned, then anyone in it couldn't see him. On that basis, he set Binky down, retaining a cautious hold of his middle, and gestured towards the translator box, blessing his stars that the child hadn't managed to lose it.

The instant Binky touched the controls, his mind exploded with input.

<<HUNGRY! WANT A DRINK! WANT SHINY THINGS! WHERE DID YOU GO?

HUNGRY!>>

And he was indeed hungry, for borne on the telepathic beam was a blast of almost overwhelming need, a level of hunger more severe than anything Peter had ever experienced. He was faint, dizzy with it, and it was only with difficulty that he refrained, once he'd got the tin of sardines open, from gobbling the lot himself. As Binky ate, however, greeding into the fish with a single-minded determination that blocked out every other thought, he felt the intensity of it diminish, and he busied himself with getting out the bottle of water. His mind had, he realised, cleared from the fog of panic and despair; finding Binky alive and, apparently, well had reduced his landscape to one of ways and means. All he had to do now was keep him away from those military nut cases until Binky's parents arrived. Then it would be up to them; they were, after all, adults. Despite everything that had occurred, Peter still cherished a belief in the power of adults to make things come out alright. He didn't count the soldiers, or Kane, as adults.

<<WANT A DRINK!>>

'Okay, okay, keep your fur on. I've got a bottle of water here. Can you drink out of the bottle?'

But Binky, it seemed, could not. Sighing, Peter poured water into his cupped hand, a little at a time, for him to lap. It wasn't very satisfactory; the water would run out between his fingers, however tightly he tried to hold them together, but little by little he managed to give Binky a drink.

The bottle felt considerably lighter than it had. He couldn't see how much was left, but it was far from full. There was a tap down at the playing fields, though. He could refill it there.

'You okay now? We need to get away from here. We're going down there, see all the trees? We can hide in there until your mum and dad come.'

<<What about my pod?>>

'You'll have to do without it. Look, Binky, you know how I told you about the bad men, right? Well those are the bad men, up at the house, and we have to hide from them until your mum and dad get here, okay?'

<<Want my pod. Want my food. Proper food. Want my toilet.>>

'You can go to the toilet in the trees. That's where I'll be going. Think of it as a camping trip.' Did Binky's people even have camping trips?

<<What's a camping trip?>>

Well, that settled that question. Peter now found himself feeling oddly light-headed, with not a care in the world, as if he were on some larky outing. They'd evaded the worst of the danger, and all they had to do now was wait. He might as well enjoy the adventure, he decided, because he was sure as eggs going to pay for it later. Even if he didn't get expelled for taking the vodka, he was going to be in a world of trouble for running away and leaving Mrs Butler to wonder what had happened to him. He ought to have left her a note, he thought. He could at least have done that, after she'd been so nice to him. The last few days, with their shared meals and Christmas, had been almost like having a real family.

They proceeded down the hill at a brisk but controlled pace, which is to say that Peter marched straight ahead, not by any means dawdling but being quite careful, because a twisted ankle would be so very inconvenient now, and Binky raced back and forth, pouncing on blades of grass and occasionally leaping into the air after a moth, for all the world as if he were really a half-grown kitten. Predictably, before they reached the bottom of the hill he was tired, and stopped abruptly to curl himself up for a nap. Peter started to wake him, but it was easier to pick him up and carry him, as the translator wafted out waves of soothing calm.

By the time he reached the wire netting fence that divided the lower playing fields from the forest, he was almost dropping with sleep himself. Partly, he supposed, because it had been a long day and a *very* long night, but also because the waves of warm, happy peacefulness from the translator were so calm, so very soothing. He'd have no trouble getting to sleep, once he could finally stop.

The loose panel was still there, held in place by a small twist of wire. He undid the wire and squeezed through, careful not to snag anything on the sharp edges. He did it up again from the other side. Hopefully there would be nothing to show his passing.

As they entered the deeper shade of the trees, Binky stirred and half woke.

<<Mummy?>>

'Soon,' Peter promised. 'She'll be here pretty soon now. We just have to be patient and wait for her. Can you do that?' It wasn't really lying, he told himself. He just hadn't given a strict meaning to 'soon'.

Under the trees, the moonlight was patchy and broken. It was hard to see where he was going, and he found it was taking all of his concentration not to trip over dead branches, which were everywhere. He pressed on, though, determined to cover as much ground as he could before they were overtaken by dawn. They needed to find a patch of dense scrub or something that would hide them from the casual observer, in case there were searchers in the forest once his absence was discovered. If only, he moaned with hindsight, he'd left a note. He could have said he was heading for town, to throw them off the scent.

All the things he might have done, should have done, bore in on him, and it became necessary to press on his top lip again. He couldn't manage it, though, with both hands occupied in carrying Binky, and he sniffed hard, blinking rapidly and drawing deep breaths, trying to get himself under control. His whole body ached with tiredness now, a deep, sharp ache like an injury. He forced himself on, one foot, the other foot, consumed with the need to find shelter, a safe hiding place. The forest, Binky's weight, his fear of the soldiers, everything melted into this single need, older than humanity, the need of a hunted animal to find a hole.

❧CHAPTER FIFTEEN☙

He never knew how much time passed before his foot, swinging forward, caught a fallen branch and he fell, panic flooding him as he didn't hit the ground but kept on falling, tumbling to rest, bruised but still clutching a protesting Binky, at the bottom of a deep hole.

Binky, woken by the fall, was fizzing.

<<WHAT HAPPENED? WHERE ARE WE? ARE WE THERE YET?>>

He couldn't see, in the dark, how deep the

hole was, or what sort of a hole it was; could not, in fact, see much of anything. But Binky was alright, and he didn't hurt, much, well not more than a few bruises and what seemed to be a grazed elbow, and the bottle hadn't broken. Peter curled himself around Binky and, like the hunted animal to which he'd been comparing himself, went fast asleep.

He woke in the dawn light, cold, thirsty, and with every part of his body screaming at him. Binky had left his side and he experienced a moment's sharp panic, but there he was, squatting at the side of the hole, intently watching something on the ground. He was a far cry from the pretty creature of yesterday; the Raven Oil had stiffened as it dried, hardening the soft fur into tacky little points to which dirt and bits of leaves adhered.

Peter looked up, for the first time taking stock of his surroundings. They seemed to have fallen into an abandoned mine working from the Gold Rush era. Peter remembered being told that the forest hereabouts was full of these, some hundreds of feet deep. That was the reason for the forest being out of bounds; you could disappear down one of the deep ones, and even if you didn't break your neck in the fall, no one would ever hear you calling for help. They had, he realised, been lucky; this hole was about three metres in diameter, and didn't seem all that deep – it would be over his head when he stood up, but the sides were rough dirt, and he thought he would be able to climb out. Most of the top of the hole was covered by leaves; he supposed it must be the top of a fallen tree, or at least a big branch. It was the hiding place he'd been seeking, presented to him as if by providence, when he might have stumbled straight past it in his exhausted state.

The first thing, he decided, was to spy out the surroundings. He was uncomfortably aware of the limited contents of his one bottle of water, and of how hot it was going to be once the sun got properly up. He didn't know how far he'd come since getting through the fence, and therefore how far he was from the tap on the edge of the football field.

A pressing need, however, made itself known as he stood up, and the location of the tap slid to second place.

'Hey, Binky. Do you need to go?'

<<WANT TO GO HOME>>

'Yes, I know, but right now, do you need to *go*? *You* know.'

<<GO BACK TO THE BIG ROOM?>> An image of the attic flashed into Peter's mind, accompanied by a wistful longing. <<WANT MY POD>>

'But do you have to *go*?' Peter gave up on politeness. 'Do you need to do wees or poos?'

They couldn't relieve themselves in this

small area; they would have to leave their hiding place for that. And he'd need to dig a hole, he supposed. It was all very hard, and he wondered if they'd have done better to hide in the attic and take their chances. Binky would have had his pod, and there might, he realised with chagrin, also have been some means of communicating with Binky's parents, once they did arrive. *If they arrive,* said a cold, prickly little voice in the back of his mind. He squashed it.

Binky apparently felt no pressing need to relieve himself. That was all to the good, thought Peter as he admonished him repeatedly to stay put until he returned. He chose the side that seemed least steep to climb out of the hole, which was not that much deeper than his head – it might be two metres or a bit less. Less, he told himself firmly. He would only have to get up a few feet before he could get an arm over the top and pull himself up. He might be able to gouge out handholds.

The dirt was hard and dry and crumbly, and

it was soon apparent that there would be no easy scooping out of handholds. He turned his attention to looking for sticking-out bits that would give his clutching fingers a little purchase, and got a little way up before the lump on which he'd pinned his hopes broke off, sending him back to the bottom, with new bruises added on top of the old.

<<ALL FALL DOWN!>> came the cheerful comment from Binky. <<IS IT A NEW GAME? LOOK, IT'S EASY!>> He proved his assertion by springing up the side of the hole, leaping from one almost invisible roughness to another, and jumping up and down exultantly at the top. <<I WON!>>

Peter sighed. The kid was so easily distracted. Just minutes before, he'd solemnly promised to stay in the hole, and there he was prancing about in full view.

'Yeah, it's a new game, but you have to take turns, alright? See, you come down now, and it's my turn, okay? Then you can have another go.' At least, he comforted himself, he wouldn't have to worry about getting Binky out of the hole.

He made it to the top on the third attempt, and lay panting for a few minutes, until the pressing call of nature brought him to his feet. He was filthy, bruised and scratched, and he ached in every muscle, and it was only the beginning of the day. To make matters worse, he now realised that he should have brought the water bottle up with him. They should both have had a big drink first, and then he'd have climbed up *with* the bottle, and then he could have gone back and filled it up from the tap before climbing back down into the hole. That might have seen them through the day in reasonable comfort. Now he was going to have to do the climb all over again.

For the first time, it struck him that he had no plan. Everything had been concentrated on getting Binky away, and then on finding somewhere to hide while they waited for Binky's parents, and he had not once stopped to think how long it might be before they came, or what he would do if they *didn't* come. He had one more tin of sardines and the vodka bottle full of water – at least he'd refilled it before going through the fence – and what was he going to do when the food ran out? He could, he supposed, manage without food for a few days himself, although the prospect was far from attractive, and in fact he was feeling pretty hungry right now, but you couldn't expect a little kid to go for days without anything to eat.

Would the soldiers give up and go away in a day or so? They would have finished searching the school by now. They couldn't be planning to hang about forever. Could they?

He scraped dirt back into the small hole he'd dug and stamped it down, and turned back towards the mineshaft, getting his bearings. It wouldn't do to get turned around. Peter had spent most of his life, apart from school, in the city, and he'd never gone in for scouting, or bird-watching, or really anything very outdoorsy. He didn't know how to find North by the sun, or what to do about snakebite, or any of that.

There was a big old burnt-out stump about half-way between the hole and the area he'd chosen for his makeshift lavatory. That would do as a landmark, he supposed. Now that it was fully light, you could see quite a long way in the forest; miles, actually, and he wished it were more like forests in books, where bandits always seemed to be able to be able to jump out from bushes, and the minute you stepped off the path you disappeared, instead of this spare landscape with huge gaps between the spindly trees, and nothing underneath except a zillion dead gum leaves. He'd have felt safer with a forest like that. What if they decided to search in here? He wouldn't have a prayer of hiding.

Binky was still in the hole, playing some game with fallen sticks that he'd built into a heap, and crooning a tuneless little song to himself. He jumped up when Peter slid down into the hole, running in manic circles around him.

<<YOU WERE GONE SO LONG! I WASN'T FRIGHTENED THOUGH. LOOK, I BUILT A HOUSE!>>

Bless his sunny nature, Peter thought. If he'd been one of those whiny kids, everything would have been so much worse. All the same, he thought they'd best stick together, not leave Binky on his own. He might have a sunny nature, but he did have one hell of a short attention span.

'Binky,' he began, 'we need to go back to where we filled up the water, to get some more water, okay?'

<<WHY?>>

'Well, because we've only got this bottle and it's going to be very hot, and what we need to do is drink as much as we can now and then I'll fill up the bottle again, and then we've got it later, for when it gets really hot.'

<<DON'T WANT A DRINK NOW.>>

It wasn't worth arguing, Peter knew. Little kids could never see ahead beyond their immediate sensations. He remembered babysitting Fiona, rolling his eyes and saying, 'Why didn't you go before we left the house?' He'd try again when they got to the fence, before he went to fill the bottle.

It wasn't long before he could see the fence; it had seemed miles and miles last night, but it was quite a short walk in the daylight. Odd scraps of litter had blown up against it, and a brightly-coloured wrapper, a chip packet or something, flapped in the breeze. Peter glanced at his wrist, only now registering that he'd forgotten to put on his watch when he'd dressed in the dark.

Binky, who had ridden most of the way clinging to Peter's shoulder atop the backpack, jumped down and scurried about in the leaves.

<<LOOK! AN ANIMAL! WHAT IS IT?>>

He had trapped a small lizard under his paw.

'It's a lizard. A skink. Let it go, it's harmless.'

<<GOOD!>> said Binky, as the end of the lizard's tail disappeared into his mouth. <<YUM! I'LL FIND US SOME MORE.>>

He busied himself stalking and pouncing among the fallen leaves. Peter, inclined at first to shudder, had second thoughts. If Binky was able to find food for himself, that was one worry less.

The school building was out of sight from here, but Peter wasn't sure *he* would be out of sight of *it*. It was a lot taller than he was. Without knowing what time it was, he didn't know if the soldiers would be awake yet. He supposed they would, though. Parker, his roommate, was in the cadets, and always moaned like anything about how early they were made to get up on camps.

Would Mrs Butler be awake yet? Had she

already discovered him missing? A hot flush of shame flooded him as he thought of how frantic she'd be. He pushed it to the back of his mind. One thing at a time, and the thing right now was the water. He sat down against a tree trunk and slid out of the backpack straps.

'Binky, come and get a drink of water. You'd like a drink now, wouldn't you?'

Binky bounded over on three legs, clutching a rather mangled skink.

<<FOUND ANOTHER! YOU HAVE THIS ONE.>>

Peter recoiled. 'No thanks, I'm not–' He remembered just in time about the translator. 'I don't feel like it right now.' That was true enough. 'You have this one. Then a big drink of water, okay?' He had been holding off himself, wanting to make sure Binky had enough, but he was almost frantic with thirst now that he wasn't concentrating on other things.

He did better with holding the water in his hand this time, having learned to keep it away from his fingers. He couldn't pour much into his palm, but then Binky didn't require very much. He lapped, Peter noticed, just like a cat. The rough tongue tickled his palm, and he giggled despite his anxiety.

Two palmsful were enough for Binky, and he was off, hunting for more lizards. Most of the bottle was still left, and finally Peter had the drink he'd been craving. He gulped it down too fast, and doubled over as his stomach cramped. The sun was warm, now, on the back of his neck. He needed to get to the tap before it got any later, but he waited a few minutes to ease the cramp and finish the bottle. Then he dashed to the loose part of the fence and was through, running to the tap, cringing as he filled the bottle and fumbled the cap back on, imagining eyes on him, perhaps weapons trained on him from up the hill.

He was sweating by the time he reached the welcome cover of the trees and sank down behind the biggest one. He felt as tired as if he'd had a long, hard day, but when he reviewed his achievements in his mind, all he'd really done was go to the lavatory and get a drink of water. And it would all have to be done again, not even tomorrow, but tonight, as soon as it got dark. The bottle wasn't going to be enough even so; he would, he knew, be desperately thirsty again before the day was half over.

Still, he comforted himself as he walked slowly back to the hole, Binky frisking around his feet and occasionally dashing off, Binky had had something to eat, so he could save the tin of sardines. His own hunger wasn't so acute with his stomach full of water, and he thought they could get through the day alright, provided they stayed in the shade. And perhaps Binky's parents would come, and once Binky was on his way home, he could go back and face the music. He'd better start thinking out what he was going to say to explain his absence. He'd give that his attention as soon as Binky went down for his nap.

With a plan of sorts, he felt better, and in fact, he was almost starting to enjoy himself.

Until he heard the helicopter.

ᏠCHAPTER SIXTEENᏠ

It roared into his awareness, the immensity of the sound laying waste to both hearing and thought, terrifying in its implication. Peter dropped to the ground, curling into as small a ball as he could manage at the base of a tree, praying its canopy would shield him from view.

'Binky!' he hissed. 'Get over here, quick! Danger!'

The thunder of the engine drowned his words, but Binky evidently still got the message through his translator, and belted over to huddle beside him.

<<IS IT THE BAD MEN IS IT IS IT>>

Moving slowly, he managed to snake an arm around Binky, holding him close, feeling the thumping of his tiny heart. Or hearts, he wondered. Doctor Who had more than one, after all.

'Don't be scared, I've got you.' He was mindful of the translator, but that wasn't actually false. 'If we keep very still, I don't think they can see us.'

<<WHAT'S THAT NOISE? IS IT A KILLING MACHINE?>>

'It's a helicopter. A flying machine. Quiet, now. Keep still.'

It seemed an eternity before the helicopter passed over and the noise started to lessen. Peter risked a look up, but couldn't see anything through the treetops. It was definitely moving away, though, in that direction. When the sound was quite faint, he got cautiously to his feet.

'It's gone, come on. We'll get back to the hole.'

Twice more they had to stop and crouch under a tree as the distant chuntering grew into a thunderous roar overhead. By the time they reached the hole and slithered down its side into the concealing shade of the overhanging tree, Peter's nerves were raw with irritation. 'Go away!' he wanted to scream, scream until his throat was raw, 'go away! Can't you leave us alone?'

Binky required constant watching to keep him under cover; Peter played some incomprehensible game with him, with bits of sticks. He suspected Binky had made up, or was still making up, the rules himself. Fiona was like it, too, and it reminded him of one of her games: insanely complicated and unpredictable. He gave up trying to understand it, and made the moves Binky told him to make. With part of his mind he listened to the helicopter, growing near, then passing over, fading away on the other side, then coming back, over and over again.

He gave Binky another drink when the sun was overhead, and took a few cautious swallows himself. He was as sparing as he could be, but when he lowered the bottle, a quarter of it was gone. There was still the afternoon and the long evening to get through before he dared go back to the tap, and the day was nowhere near as hot yet as it would be.

The helicopter seemed to have moved farther off; he could barely hear it now. Binky seemed to be slowing down; he hadn't corrected Peter's gameplay for some time, and there was a quietness to the translator stream that suggested he might soon be thinking about a nap. He was taking longer and longer between moves, and presently he moved over next to Peter and curled up in his lap. Just like a real cat, thought Peter, resisting the urge to stroke him. Carefully he stretched his legs out and leaned back against the side of the hole. His feet were in the sun, but he'd pull his knees up if he heard the chopper coming back. He reviewed his situation.

He'd got Binky out of immediate danger. That was good, but there were problems with surviving out here. The constant need for water was going to be the biggest one, but food came a close second. Binky had surprised him by catching his own food, but that couldn't be relied on; what if the lizards ran out, or he lost interest in hunting? Then, there were his own needs. He couldn't go without food forever.

Supposing they managed about the food and water, what then? He didn't know how long it would take Binky's parents to receive the beacon signal. *Or,* whispered a cold, scratchy voice at the back of his mind, *whether they'll receive it at all.* What if the beacon was out of order? Don't be silly, he chided himself. You heard it through the translator, remember? They'll hear it, and they'll come. He clung to this as a drowning man clings to a bit of driftwood. Binky's parents would come, and they would take Binky home and then everything would be all right.

Sustained by this comforting thought, he had almost dropped off to sleep when a new thought jolted him awake, with such force that he jerked upright, eliciting a grumble of protest from the sleeping Binky.

The beacon, to which Binky's parents would no doubt be heading, was still in the pod. In the school. Surrounded by enemy soldiers.

He wondered, with faint surprise, when he had started thinking of the Australian army as the enemy. *When they started acting like it,* he answered himself. *When that Kane threatened to burn me with a cigarette. When they pointed their guns at the car. They changed then.*

No, he thought, that wasn't quite right. The soldiers and the government men hadn't changed; they must have been like that already. It was he who had changed. He saw things differently, now. Would the world ever go back to how it had been, he wondered, knowing that it couldn't, grieving for the loss even as he rejoiced in his clearer sight.

That wasn't the problem now, though. The problem was that Binky's mum and dad were heading straight into the enemy stronghold, where they would be either shot and killed or, more likely, captured and done who knew what to in a laboratory somewhere. And there'd be no one who even knew who they were or what had happened to them.

Except me.

And it came to him how easily he, Peter, could disappear.

The helicopter was back, somewhere to the – what direction was it, anyway? The direction away from the school. The sound approached and retreated, approached and retreated, but it was not coming close, as it had done before. They must be searching a new area. That was a small comfort, but what was he going to do?

In books, he'd have discovered an abandoned woodsman's cottage by now. There'd be stores of food, and water in a well, and firewood stacked by the door. Or there'd be a kindly hermit or wizard, who would have all kinds of solutions to everything. He closed his eyes, longing to be able to lay his problems in the hands of some wise adult who would sort everything out. It was very warm now, and the droning sound of the helicopter in the distance was really rather pleasant....

He woke all at once, his heart pounding, his mouth dry, echoes from his dream pounding in his head, something about a death sentence, in the booming tones that had so often sounded in the nastier of his nightmares. The light was wrong, flatter, and the solid weight of Binky was gone from his lap. He flailed in panic, reaching out blindly till his vision cleared and he realised the pounding in his head wasn't only from the dream.

The sun had shifted position while he slept,

and its slanting rays had slipped under the sheltering leaves. He'd been sleeping with the full blast of the summer sun on his head and the back of his neck, and now his head was a landscape of pain, spikes of agony thrusting skyward from a field of dull ache. It hurt even to shake his head, and his vision was blurry, his eyes sore and scratchy. He pinched the back of his hand, and watched in dull, remote dismay as the sharp peak of skin slowly subsided. He should be more alarmed, he knew, at this evidence of dehydration, but it all seemed like too much trouble.

The bottle of water was also lying in the sun, and was hot to the touch. Great, a hot drink, just what he needed. He unscrewed the cap and took a cautious sip. It wasn't so bad if you pretended it was tea, although he could still taste the sickly taint of the vodka. He drank a careful quarter of the bottle, taking slow sips, shivering with pleasure despite the heat of it.

Binky had shifted into the deepest part of the

overhang, where the shade was thickest and the sun, even at this angle, didn't penetrate. Should he wake him, Peter wondered, and get him to drink some water? He looked so peaceful, but dehydration could kill. He settled for running a hand lightly down Binky's back. The child curled tighter and emitted a contented murmur through the translator; the feeling was of comfort and happiness, so he left him to sleep, thinking how useful the device would be to vets. Imagine if you could know exactly how much pain a sick animal was in, and where the pain was, and so on!

The worst thing about this whole situation, he decided as the long afternoon wore on, was the sheer boredom of it. It made him want to be reckless; apart from his burning thirst, the need to do something, anything, was like a fire in his mind. Several times he caught himself thinking it wouldn't hurt to go for more water, that they wouldn't be looking at the playing fields, and as often he stopped himself, concentrating sternly on the memory of those gun muzzles pointed at Mrs Butler's car. If only he'd brought something to read, or even his watch. Anything at all that would get his mind off how thirsty he was, and how grotty he was starting to feel. Like most children, he had been accustomed to his daily shower chiefly by the force of custom, but now he experienced it as a visceral need; his skin felt grimy and crawly, and his clothes were clammy and somehow sticky against his skin. His fingernails were black, there was a foul taste in his mouth, his head itched and he was uncomfortably aware that he had not washed his hands after going to the lavatory.

He was jolted out of a daydream involving a deep, hot bath, a bar of lemon-scented soap and a nailbrush by the sound of gunfire from up the hill. They were shooting at something again; at least it wasn't Binky this time. Unlike the other night, though, the shooting went on and on and on, and it wasn't just normal shots – from the movies, he recognised the shuddering roar of automatic fire. His headache was a spike of molten steel, lancing through his brain.

The gunfire went on and on. Binky woke from his nap crying, and had to be reassured. Peter cursed the truth requirement of the translator even as he blessed its ability to work even in the barrage of noise. He couldn't say everything was okay. Everything wasn't okay. Nothing was okay. They were probably going to die.

'Try to stay calm,' he finally sent. It didn't seem to help.

&CHAPTER SEVENTEEN&

When the noise stopped, it was quite sudden. The silence struck him like a blow, and he reeled sideways. Binky, who had crawled into his lap and curled into a tight, shivering ball, his little hands clutching Peter's shirt, fell off and sprawled in the dirt.

<<OW, YOU TIPPED ME OFF.>>

'Sorry, Binky,' he said, lifting the child back into his lap. 'I lost my balance for a second, I didn't mean to.' His voice sounded loud in the silence, and he dropped to a whisper.

'It's nearly dark. I'll go and fill up the water soon, okay? Do you want to come, or stay here?'

Binky elected to go, and could only be restrained with difficulty from springing up the side of the hole. Peter grabbed him and hauled him back. 'Not yet. We've got to wait till it's properly dark. There's still some water left in the bottle, if you want a drink.'

<<NOT A DRINK. I'M HUNGRY. WANT A LIZARD.>>

'Well, find one in here.'

<<I ATE ALL THEM, WHILE YOU WERE SLEEPING. WANT ANOTHER. I'M HUNGRY.>>

Peter ground his teeth. There was, he knew, no point in trying to reason with a child as young as Binky once he really wanted something. He still had the can of sardines, but he dreaded opening it. Once those were gone, they had no more food, and he was so hungry himself; he had determined to save them for Binky, but he didn't know if he could resist gobbling the lot himself once he smelt them. He forced his mind away from the memory of the strong, oily taste, once despised but now the most desirable thing in the world.

Inspiration struck. 'Binky, see that little hole over there? It looks a bit like a mouse hole. They're yummy. If you sit very quietly and watch the hole, one might come out.' He felt like a traitor, but nothing he'd said was really untrue, and it might keep Binky occupied for the half an hour or so that he estimated remained before it would be dark enough to venture out. He settled back to watch Binky watching the hole.

The silence wasn't as complete as he'd thought at first. Now that his ears had adjusted to the absence of the pounding gunfire, he could hear the trees rustling in a slight breeze, and an occasional birdcall. As he listened to the sounds of the evening, he started to feel almost relaxed, until a new sound, horrible in its incongruity, sent the blood rushing from his face and the bottom dropping from his stomach.

He could hear footsteps.

They were some way off; how far, he couldn't tell, but the swishing sound of footfalls on dead leaves and the occasional twig snapping was quite clear, and couldn't be very far distant. He scrunched more deeply under the cover of the fallen tree, reaching a frantic arm to grab his backpack and the bottle. You got careless after a while, he thought. You couldn't keep up being full-on frightened for long. You got used to it, and then you got careless.

He lay still, straining to pick up the faint sounds. They were moving away from him, he thought, or hoped.

Time passed. The light began to fade, the trees overhead losing their colour and standing out black against the sky. Binky gave up on the hole, and settled for a nap, curled into a ball under Peter's arm, one foot digging into his ribs. He tried to wriggle away from the small discomfort, but stopped when Binky shifted restlessly and the smooth flow of tranquillity from the translator stuttered. Let the kid sleep. Poor little guy.

More time passed. The moon made an appearance. Peter's thirst was now a raging fire, impossible to control. He had to get more water, no matter what. He drained the bottle, now mercifully cooled, and considered the sleeping Binky. He didn't want to wake the child, but cringed away from the idea of leaving him sleeping and unprotected. You didn't leave little kids by themselves. You just didn't. With regret, he nudged Binky gently.

'It's time to go for water,' he whispered. 'Wake up.'

Binky stiffened and scrunched into a tighter ball.

<<GO AWAY, I'M SLEEPY. DON'T WANT TO GO.>>

Peter sighed. 'You have to come, it's not safe out here at night by yourself.' There was nothing as far as he could see that would be a threat to Binky, but there was a very real danger that Binky would get bored, or have a bright idea, and wander off and get lost. He thought longingly of the real world. If they were at home, you'd have a pusher for a child this age. He'd often seen little kids sitting happily out for the count in pushers, while their mothers chatted or shopped. Some ladies carried their babies in bag things strapped to their backs.

Then he saw the backpack.

It was quite big enough, he thought. Binky was, after all, only about as big as a small cat.

'Look, Binky. You can ride in the backpack, and I'll carry you.'

It worked quite well, in fact. After a few grumbles, Binky settled down in the bottom of the backpack and went back to sleep. The wash of tranquil contentment through

Peter's mind made him want to lie down and sleep himself, and he had to pinch himself once or twice to maintain his alertness. He wondered briefly if he should get Binky to turn the translator off, but the possibility of needing to communicate instantly should they be discovered made this, he felt, a bad idea.

The walk back to the fence wasn't as easy, somehow, as it had been that morning. He was stiff from lying on the ground, and tired with a deep, grinding tiredness that ached in his bones and stung his eyes. His bed at school seemed a long, long way off, in both time and space, and it startled him to reflect that it had only been a little more than twenty-four hours ago that he'd left the school for Mrs Butler's cottage. If only he could be back at school, taking a long, hot shower in the big school bathroom, surrounded by clouds of steam and the strong, distinctive smell of the school soap. Or at the long tables in the school dining room, devouring a boring, carb-laden (delicious) school dinner. Or stretched out to sleep in the hard, narrow (soft, luxurious) school bed, listening to Parker snoring. If he ever got back there, he promised himself, he'd be nicer to Parker, and would not short-sheet his bed on the first night back from holidays, as he'd been planning to do.

A flash of light caught his eye, interrupting his reverie. Great, he thought. Just great. A thunderstorm was all they needed, out here in the bush with no shelter anywhere. He waited for the thunder, counting seconds, but heard nothing and gave up when he reached twenty. It must be very far away; with luck, the rain wouldn't reach them.

There was another flash in his peripheral vision, over there on the right. Peter stared upwards. The stars glittered bright and clear, and the moon floated serene on a dark sea of silence. Funny that there didn't seem to be any clouds.

Another flash, longer this time, and he was able to pinpoint its location, not up in the sky at all but down near the ground, and then he froze in horror as the angle of it shifted and he saw the beam and recognised the light source as a torch, and heard again the small crash of a footfall. He felt Binky stirring in the backpack, wriggling and kicking. The walking motion soothed small children, said the knowledge drifting back to him from a long-ago documentary. Keep moving, he told himself, mentally shouting to drown the voices of panic that yammered and gibbered in his mind. They'd come to the fence any minute. They'd fill up the bottle, have a good big drink and get back to the hole, he told himself, willing the panic to subside. Just stay calm. You've got to have water.

He set off again, moving quickly but as quietly as possible, but keeping an eye out for more flashes. It slowed him down a little, as he didn't dare take a step without looking where he was stepping, but he fell into a rhythm – step, step, look around, step, step... and it seemed as if he was going to make it to the fence without incident.

Until he heard a muffled exclamation, and turned and saw the eye of the torch pointing directly at him.

He was already running as he tried to reason with himself, running blindly without caring about the direction, fully panicking even as he tried to make himself believe the torch beam couldn't have possibly reached that far, couldn't really have exposed him, stark against the dark forest, like a rabbit caught in headlights. Behind him, he heard the crashing of footsteps, bigger footsteps than his own. The soldiers had found him, and he cringed, imagining the bullet crashing into his spine, and then he remembered that Binky was on his back, right in the path of the bullet he expected any second.

Binky, woken by the jolting motion of his running, was squawking with outrage.

<<STOP SHAKING ME. DO NOT WANT!>>

'It's going to be okay,' Peter muttered under his breath, knowing the translator would pick it up despite the low volume. 'Just keep your head down and hang on.' He hoped the translator had managed the reassurance he'd intended. He wasn't sure how true it was, because right at this moment he didn't think it was going to be okay, at all, ever again.

As he ran, he tried to pull the backpack forward, to get it in front where it would be shielded by his body, but it was hopeless, the straps too short to get it around. He didn't dare try to get one arm out of it running, in case he dropped it; he would have to stop if he wanted to move it to the front, and he couldn't stop, mustn't stop running... his breath sounded loud and harsh in his ears, and down the tunnel of time came the voice of Mr Woodrow, reminding him to control his breathing, so as not to run out of wind.

Were they gaining? Peter couldn't hear anything over the sounds of his own feet and his own breathing, now a tortured rasp. He sped on in the dark, heading for some imagined haven, somewhere, anywhere, he could hide and get his breath.

With a shock of cold horror it came to him that the forest was full of holes, some quite deep, and not all were harmless, like the one he'd fallen into the previous night. Old mineshafts, some going down hundreds of feet, the boys had been warned, and that was the reason for the tall fence that encircled the school grounds, to keep the boys out of the forest. Stupid, stupid to run blindly like this in the dark. He dropped back to a jog. The pursuing feet seemed farther off, but he couldn't be sure. He risked a look back, but could see nothing. And then the world gave a sickening lurch and he crashed to the ground, searing pain screaming from his ankle and Binky screaming protests and terror from his back.

Pain rolled over him like a wave, and for a few seconds he was blind, deaf, completely undone. Then he was bathed in light, and looking up, he saw it descending above him, a wide circle of brilliant white light, and heard a deep, strong humming sound that seemed to vibrate in his bones until all sound suddenly ceased, and his vision blinked out as if someone, somewhere had flicked a switch.

ଌCHAPTER EIGHTEENଔ

His consciousness returned slowly, drifting in like mist, his senses returning one by one. He could hear voices, murmuring too softly for him to make out the words. Then his twisted ankle throbbed sharply, and the sounds clicked into focus.

((...caught him in the edge of the camouflage field.))

@@...give him something for the pain...@@

((...better not until we do the bioscan.))

<<BAD MANS! I SAVED US!>>

A wash of love, and relief, and satisfaction, tinged with a faint hue of laughter, and Peter understood that he was hearing all this through the translator. Wondering, he opened his eyes.

They were like Binky, and yet not like; still catlike, but you would never mistake these people for cats, he thought. For one thing, they were much bigger, about the size of a large dog, but it wasn't so much that as their general air; there was a stillness about them, a quiet dignity that made him feel very young and untidy, and for all their four legs and fur there was no way they could be seen as anything but people, and very grown-up people at that.

The one on the left had to be Binky's mother. That was obvious from the way Binky was pressed up against her, clinging to her with his little hands. A stream of bliss poured steadily through the translator, forming a backdrop to the input, clearer and somehow sharper, of his parents. That wave of love had been his mother, and a quieter stream came from the other being, who, Peter assumed, had to be his father. There wasn't much content to it, somehow. He must be one of those quiet men, like Peter's own father.

((Ah, you're awake. How do you feel? We caught you in the edge of the camouflage field. Couldn't be avoided, I'm afraid. Can you stand? Any nausea or double vision?))

'I think I'm okay,' Peter stammered. He sat up, rather carefully, but apart from a slight dizziness, he felt normal enough. He scrambled to his feet, noticing for the first time the bright light; it was like daylight, a bit. 'Listen, you need to turn that light off, you could see that for miles, they'll be after you.' He didn't know how to explain the hostility of the government men and the army. For the first time, he felt ashamed. This was his country, no, his world, and they had visitors from the stars, and they were *shooting* at them.

@@Sit back down. I need to do a bioscan.@@ There was an oddly familiar feeling about this being's translator stream, and it came to him with a kind of numb recognition that she sounded (felt, or whatever word you used when it was really telepathic communication) quite like his Aunty Jean, that time he had been in bed with 'flu. A sort of bossy mixture of softness and fierceness, as if on some level she was saying, 'you poor boy, but don't you dare get out of that warm bed.'

'But the soldiers– they were shooting at Binky before, and there was a lot of shooting this afternoon–'

((Yes, that was us.)) A hint of amusement, faintly supercilious. ((Primitive projectile weaponry. Nothing to worry about.))

@@Don't worry. No one can see us now. That's what the camouflage field is for.@@

She had taken some kind of device from what Peter now saw was a kind of harness, with pockets of various sizes. The other person had one, too. Clothes must not be a thing in their society. Perhaps if you had fur, you never developed the need for them. Kindly but firmly admonished, he kept very, very still while she ran the device over him, not quite touching. He thought when it passed over his bare arm that he could feel a faint tingling.

@@Don't worry, it won't hurt you. There, all finished.@@ She peered at the device. @@You seem to be undamaged. Do you always have a very low [burst of static]?@@

'I'm sorry,' said Peter. 'I don't know what that is.'

((Do you need a drink?)) The other being, whom Peter had designated in his mind as Binky's father, looked over his wife's shoulder, and a burst of rapid communication that Peter couldn't understand passed back and forth between them. ((Water?))

Peter was all at once aware of his burning

thirst, the dryness in his mouth and eyes. Water! Binky's mother patted his shoulder and whisked away. He turned to watch her go, and saw for the first time what was behind him.

Perhaps twenty feet long, the ovoid craft gleamed softly golden. From an opening in its side, a ramp protruded to the ground. They had landed in a small clearing, and the ship looked weirdly incongruous against the gum trees. But it was beautiful, its proportions elegant and somehow perfect, in the way that an egg is perfect, not allowing the possibility of any other shape. Peter drew in a deep, deep breath. No one in the world, he realised, had seen this, except him.

Binky's mother emerged from the ship with a tray slung round her neck. She padded down the ramp and set down the tray next to him, then settled herself again beside her partner, curling her tail neatly around her feet. Binky, beside her, had collapsed into deep sleep in the sudden way of small children.

He inspected the tray. There was a squat flask of what looked like glass, and a small bowl of the same material, and another bowl containing what might have been dried fruit. Binky's mother poured water into the bowl and handed it to him with a little movement that might have been a ceremonial bow; he tried to imitate it as he took the bowl.

Don't drink too fast, he reminded himself. He'd been caught that way before. Throw too much cold water down your throat too quickly, when you were hot and thirsty, and your stomach would cramp, racking you with agony for several minutes. It had happened to him just that morning, and the water hadn't even been cold, not like this water, which was beautifully chilled. It was hard to restrain himself from guzzling, with the cool, delicious sensation of it going into his body; he thought he could actually feel it soaking into his parched tissues, and it made him almost dizzy with pleasure. He forced himself to drink slowly, taking tiny sips and letting it trickle down his throat, but the bowl was soon empty; it was, he guessed, about the size of a teacup, or a little smaller. He sighed, and looked hopefully at the flask. You mustn't ever ask for things in people's houses, Aunty Jean had drummed into him. It was unspeakably rude, because they might not have enough of whatever it was, and you could embarrass them. He supposed the spaceship was like a house, for the purposes of manners; he was, after all, their guest.

Thinking about manners recalled him to his other obligations. 'I'm sorry,' he said. 'I should have introduced myself. My name's Peter Fotheringay. I've been taking care of Binky.'

Again the warm rush of love and relief, coloured with gratitude.

@@Indeed, Binky has been telling us. We are so thankful to you. But I am remiss; I am Araima, and my partner is Ngaurr.@@ She refilled his bowl, and he sipped gratefully, wishing the bowl were bigger, eyeing the flask.

((We honour your care for our child,)) Ngaurr added. ((But can you explain the situation here? Why did those people fire projectiles at us? We are scientists, cleared only for botanical investigation. We ought not to have landed on an inhabited planet, it is true, but we did not threaten anyone.))

Peter didn't know what to say. The bowl was empty again – how had that happened? He set it down with a small pang of regret.

'See, people here, they don't know about other kinds of people, from other planets and that. I mean we do, sort of, but it's just stories, books and movies, made-up stuff. No one's ever actually come here from another planet. Lots of people think we're the only sentient race there is. And in the movies, when there's aliens, they're usually the bad guys, like they'll be coming here to kill us and stuff. And those people who shot at you – they're the army, but it was Border Force who brought them in. They're part of the government, and their thing is to stop anyone from coming into Australia, that's our country. See, other countries in the world, some of them are pretty awful, they've got evil governments or they've been bombed and stuff, and people come here from those places to be safe and make a better life, and Border Force kill them and lock them up and stuff.' He was making a hash of it, he knew, and faltered into silence in the face of the astonishment and disbelief, and the horrified, nauseated disgust, trickling through the translator.

❧CHAPTER NINETEEN☙

In the little pool of silence that followed, Araima refilled the bowl. She did it with a sort of automatic courtesy, but Peter could feel the distress leaking from her.

@@They would have killed Binky?@@

'Well, they were shooting at him last night, but they thought he was a cat. See, that's why I put the black stuff on him, to make him look like a cat if anyone saw him from a distance. A cat's an animal that we have here, and Binky sort of looks a bit like one if you don't look too close, except for his colour, see animals here never are green. So I thought he'd be safer, the Border Force guys had already been sniffing around.' He stopped himself, not wanting to reveal just how dreadful Kane and his associate had been, or his suspicions of what would have happened to Binky if caught.

((So you disguised him, and then you brought him out here, away from them?))

'Yeah, I ran away, basically. I'm going to be in so much trouble.'

@@Why trouble? May you not leave your home?@@

'It's not my home, it's a school. We're not allowed out of the school grounds without permission.' It occurred to him that they didn't know he wasn't an adult. 'I'm only twelve, you know.'

Shock and concern. The translator, he knew, would give the sense of relative maturity along with the age, as it had done when he first met Binky.

((But why disguise him as a cat, if they were going to shoot at a cat?))

'I didn't *know* they'd shoot at him. No one shoots at cats. They live in people's houses, they're pets, we don't kill them. These guys – they're all wrong, it's not how they're supposed to be...' he trailed off miserably.

((But you thought they'd shoot at him if they *didn't* think he was a cat?))

'Yeah, probably. Or worse.'

((Worse?))

Peter was starting to feel like an insect under a microscope.

'I don't *know* what. But if they got him in a laboratory, if scientists got him... they might experiment on him, hurt him... I don't know, really, but it wouldn't be anything good.'

There was a long silence, during which Peter identified shock, horror and disgust in the translator feed. His face felt flushed, his nose had stuffed up and his throat hurt. He realised with horror that he was going to cry, and jabbed frantically at his top lip with his knuckle.

@@Stop harassing him, Ngaurr. He's only a child. Here, eat some of these, Peter Fotheringay. They're Binky's favourites.@@

She pushed the bowl of whatever it was towards him, and refilled the water bowl again. She was a mother alright, Peter thought, comparing her with a small pang to his own glamorous, party-going mother. He'd better eat something. It always made grown-ups happy if you did, if they were trying to be nice to you. He picked up a piece of stuff, put it in his mouth, bit down... and then spat it out, only just managing to turn his head away from Araima as he spat, doubling over and heaving. The taste was beyond awful, worse, far worse than Binky's brown pellets. It seemed both putrid and chemical at the same time. Luckily he had only water in his stomach; he managed to keep it down. Most of it, anyway.

'I don't think this kind of food is good for humans,' he choked out, hoping that was tactful enough.

Araima had refilled the drinking bowl again, amid murmurs of concern and apology, and he swilled water around his mouth, forcing himself to swallow it, trying to wash away the vile taste.

@@I'll get you something else.@@

'No, please don't bother, I'm really not hungry,' lied Peter.

Araima fixed him with what, even with her alien features, he could tell was the look an adult gives a child who has been caught in an outright lie, and a silly one, at that. He'd forgotten about the translator's truth filter. What had she heard, part of him wondered, even as most of him sank into his shoes. Surprisingly, the sterner Ngaurr came to his rescue.

((There's no time, Rai. We need to be going. The camouflage field won't help us if they walk right up to it. There's that one blundering about in the trees, remember.))

@@We could take him with us...@@

((Don't be silly, Rai. What would he do, the only one of his species? What kind of life could he have? It's not like that litter of [burst of static] you rescued. He's a person. People need their own kind. You don't even know if he could live on World. Just because we can breathe this air, doesn't mean he can breathe ours, remember.))

'It's okay,' Peter interjected, feeling a bit sad that he wouldn't get to ride in their ship. 'I'll be alright. I'm just a kid, they won't do anything. I'll say I got scared and ran off. They can't really do anything to me.' He did believe that, sort of. He hoped.

Araima slipped the tray's straps over her head and started to gather up the bowls.

@@Five [burst of static], yes?@@

She bounded up the ramp and disappeared inside the ship. Left alone with Ngaurr,

Peter couldn't think of anything to say. He stared down at his filthy sneakers, scuffing his toe in the dirt. Then a thought occurred to him.

'Where do you come from, Ngaurr? Can you see your star from here?'

Ngaurr's whiskers twitched in a way that, with Binky, Peter had come to associate with happiness. He supposed it to be the equivalent of a smile.

((Indeed you can.)) He raised a hand and pointed to the sky. ((Do you see that line of three stars, close together in a straight line?))

'Sure, Orion's Belt.'

((Up and to the right of that, there's a very bright star. Do you see it? The really bright one?))

'Sirius? You come from Sirius?' Peter started to laugh. 'That's so funny!'

((Funny? Why?))

'It's part of a constellation we call Canis

Major. The big dog. And your people, well, to us you kind of look like cats, a bit.'

((I don't understand.))

Peter shook his head, still laughing. 'I think it's really only funny to a human. It's stupid really.'

Araima emerged from the hatch. @@We're ready to go, Ngaurr.@@

Suddenly it all seemed very real. They were going to leave, Peter realised, they were going and they'd never come back.

'Could I say goodbye to Binky?'

@@Of course. We'll be inside, won't we, Ngaurr? I say, *won't we*, Ngaurr?@@

Binky was still sleeping soundly. Peter squatted down next to him. The poor kid must be exhausted, he thought, smiling fondly. All the excitement, and not enough to eat really, and probably short of sleep, and worst of all, he was out of his routine. And then the big emotional thing of seeing his mum and dad. Well, he'd be alright. He'd have forgotten about all this soon. It was really kindest to let him sleep. And yet he found himself running a hand gently down Binky's back. The child stirred, muttering, and through the translator the wash of tranquillity grew thin for a second, then rolled back in. He leant down, close to Binky's ear, and spoke softly.

'Wake up, Binky. I've come to say goodbye. You're going home now, with your mum and dad.'

<<PETER!>> Binky surged up, wrapping skinny arms around his neck and leaping onto his chest. Peter wrapped his arms around the child.

'I have to go, Binky. This is goodbye. You're going home.'

<<YOU COME TOO.>>

'I can't come, Binky. I have to stay and finish school.'

<<WILL YOU COME AND SEE ME?

YOU CAN COME AND PLAY AT OUR HOUSE.>>

Peter sighed. 'Maybe one day, okay?'

<<COME SOON. I'VE GOT A NEW [burst of static]. YOU CAN PLAY WITH IT.>>

'Just as soon as I can.' It wasn't a lie.

<<TOMORROW?>>

'Not tomorrow. I have stuff to do tomorrow.'

<<THE DAY AFTER TOMORROW?>>

'As soon as I can.'

<<PROMISE?>>

'If I can. Don't worry, I know where you live.'

He bent slowly and set Binky on the ground. 'Go on now. Your Mum and Dad are waiting.' He watched as Binky scampered up the ramp without a backwards look. That was how little kids were, he reminded himself.

Araima came out and padded up to him. @@We're leaving now. We'll turn off the camouflage field, so you won't get caught in the perimeter again. I'll always be grateful to you, Peter Fotheringay. Your name will not be forgotten in our family.@@

'It was nothing, Araima. I liked taking care of him, really. He's a great kid.'

He stood and watched as the hatchway closed and the ramp was drawn back into the ship. The subliminal hum intensified, and there was a brief flash, like sheet lightning. That was the camouflage field going off, he supposed.

The hum built to a faint scream that was almost, but not quite, consciously audible. The golden craft rose slowly and silently into the air, clearing the surrounding treetops by what looked like less than a foot. Ngaurr must be one hell of a pilot. Or perhaps it was Araima. He kept his eyes on it until it went suddenly blurry. That must be the camouflage field going back on, he told himself.

'Goodbye, Binky,' he murmured. 'I wouldn't have missed it for the world.'

❧CHAPTER TWENTY☙

P eter shivered in the suddenly chilly air. It must be very late; the moon was setting, sinking below the trees. He'd lost track, watching Binky's ship recede. It hadn't been more than a couple of minutes before it was indistinguishable from all the other pinpoints of light in the night sky, but he had remained standing, staring after it, kidding himself that he knew which one it was. He wiped his nose – the cold had made it run – and turned away, his mind empty. He was so tired, so very tired, and more than anything he longed to return to the hole and sleep.

But there was the music to be faced.

He squared his shoulders and started walking back. He wasn't even sure which way it was, after his mindless, panicked flight, but the moon was in *that* direction, and it was setting, so it made sense that part, at least, of the fence would be *that* way, and he could follow it along until he found the hole. Then he'd walk back up the hill, and hope he didn't get shot. He was so tired that he found he couldn't care very deeply about it. He'd done his best, and he'd got Binky away safely, and the future yawned dark and empty and inconsequential. He'd have to apologise, and make excuses, just as he'd done so many times in his life, although never for an infraction so serious as running away.

He limped on his twisted ankle, head down, one foot in front of the other, with only one thought in his mind – to get back to the cottage. There was Mrs Butler to be faced, and he shied away from thinking about that. There were, of course, the soldiers at the school, with their loaded weapons, and he would somehow have to get past them, but they seemed trivial now, almost beside the point, and he couldn't bring himself to care very much about them. Even his nagging hunger had faded away, replaced by a faint nausea. He plodded on, not thinking, not seeing, until he slammed into something in the dark and found himself enveloped in soft, perfumed warmth.

He was so startled and horrified he couldn't move, until the hushed babble of words sorted itself out. It seemed an age since he'd listened to human speech, or had any communication that didn't come via the telepathic translator, and it was a minute or two before the sounds slid into focus, and he realised he was being clutched to the ample bosom of Mrs Butler.

'...thank God you're okay. You *are* okay, aren't you? Peter? Are you hurt or anything?'

Peter struggled free and blinked up at her. Not as up as usual; she somehow wasn't as tall as she was supposed to be, and looking down he saw that she'd replaced her stilettoes with sneakers. Who would have thought Mrs Butler even owned anything as plain as sneakers?

'Mrs Butler!' he blurted out. 'What are you doing here?'

'Looking for you, of course, what did you think? You just vanished into thin air, and I knew you couldn't have got out by the road, they've a guard on the gate.'

'But why here? I mean, how did you know to look in the forest?'

'I didn't, not really. I was wandering round the grounds, and I saw the tap had been used at the bottom of the playing field – it was wet all around, you could see someone'd been using it. So I thought you'd been down there in the last day, and then I saw the hole in the fence, so I went through it. It was just luck, really, that I found you. I'd been searching for hours. And here you are, you poor little lamb. You look beat. Can you manage up the hill? Do you want to rest?'

This was all wrong, Peter thought fuzzily. He'd been expecting a tiger of wrath, not this motherly fussing.

'I'm really sorry,' he began.

'Never mind, it doesn't matter now. I'm just so glad you're safe. I've been so worried, Peter. I didn't know what to think. I went to call you for breakfast and you were gone. Just gone.'

Her voice had a forlorn, plaintive sound, and Peter felt, if possible, even worse.

'I should have left a note. I'm really sorry, Mrs Butler, I didn't mean to worry you, I just didn't think….' She had turned and started walking, and he limped jerkily after her, still apologising. She didn't reply, and after a while he faltered into silence.

She didn't speak again until they reached the fence, and then it was only to say that she was quite sure they ought to turn right, rather than left. In silence they came to the hole in the fence; in silence they passed through it.

It was very late now, and the stars were beginning to fade. Soon the birds would start up.

'We'll have to hurry, now,' said Mrs Butler. 'Not long till dawn, and military people are early risers. Not that this lot are exactly professional, mind.'

Peter thought that was a bit unfair, since they were benefitting from the soldiers' slackness. 'Would you rather they were more professional, then?' he asked. 'Shot us more efficiently, kind of thing?'

'Don't be silly, Peter. If they were professional, they wouldn't have been shooting at all. Blazing away like Stormtroopers after a Jedi. Idiots. You heard them yesterday afternoon. I was terrified, and with you out God knows where…'

'I'm really sorry,' said Peter again. He had lagged behind Mrs Butler a little way, struggling up the hill on his twisted ankle. She turned to look back.

'Hurry up, Peter, what are you – oh, you're limping! What have you done, twisted your ankle?'

'Yeah, I tripped on a root when I was running away from – well, I suppose it must have been you, actually, that was you with the torch, wasn't it?'

'Oh, Peter. Here, lean on me. Or I could give you a piggy-back?'

'No, that's fine,' said Peter. He wasn't going to be carried like some little kid. 'I'm okay.'

She slipped her arm around him. 'Here, let me take some of your weight on this side. We'll have a look at it when we get back. You've been very brave through this whole thing, I must say.'

'Yeah, running away, that's real brave.' Already, he realised, he was falling into the view of events that he would present when asked. For a little while there, he'd been proud, proud that he'd saved Binky, against appalling odds and without help.

Mrs Butler didn't say anything, but her arm tightened around him.

The school was dark and silent, brooding atop the hill like a great animal. They slipped past it in the predawn light, skirting the kitchen gardens and dropping to hands and knees behind the shrubbery. The final hundred yards down the front lawn were the hardest – with their goal in sight, Peter found it almost physically difficult to turn his back on the school, and he forced himself to run, heedless of the spikes of pain from his ankle, his spine crawling as he imagined a bullet smashing into it. He reached the cottage before Mrs Butler, and clung to the verandah post, panting, tears forming as all the pain he'd ignored smashed into his ankle at once.

Inside, the cottage was dim and warm, the closed, curtained room retaining the heat of yesterday. Peter staggered to the sofa and collapsed, his ankle screaming. Mrs Butler, after some exclamations of horror (Oh my God! You're white as a sheet! Put your foot up and get your shoe off!) bustled off to the kitchen. He lay back against the cushions and closed his eyes, his nerves vibrating. It seemed incredible that it had only been less than forty-eight hours that he'd had dinner here, and gone quietly up to bed.

Mrs Butler came back in with a large bowl.

'Here, Peter, put your foot in this. Get your shoe off, I told you to take your shoe off, come on.'

There were ice cubes floating in the bowl. Peter thought it was too late for ice, but he didn't want to argue. He got his shoe off, not without some pain, and peeled down his sock. The ankle was twice its normal size; it even looked painful.

'Go on, get it in there, it won't bite.'

Where was all the sympathy now? He didn't want to soak in ice water. He wanted a hot bath, and something to eat, and bed. He dipped his toe into the water, then carefully lowered his foot. It actually felt quite good. His head felt swimmy with tiredness. Outside, a magpie burst into liquid song. He'd been up all night, he realised with dull wonder; there was light seeping in around the edges of the curtains. Mrs Butler had gone away, and was clattering about in the kitchen. Presently, the smell of frying bacon drifted in.

Breakfast was sheer heaven. Peter sat and devoured bacon, fried eggs, tomatoes and baked beans. By the time he slowed down, Mrs Butler was on her third cup of coffee. She sat, quiet and somehow comfortable, watching him with an unreadable expression. When he finally sat back, feeling as if his stomach might burst, she took his plate and cleared the table, still without speaking, and sat back down.

'Well, Peter, I think a hot bath and then bed, don't you? Did you sleep at all, last night?'

'Not really. I slept a bit during the day, and the night before... it's all a bit of a blur, honestly.'

'Well, go and sleep now. Better leave the bath till you wake up. We don't want you falling asleep and drowning. You can have a quick shower, then into bed with you. Can you manage alright up the stairs?'

'Mrs Butler, I–'

'Never mind that, we can talk when you've rested. Off you go.'

He wanted to stay under the shower all day, letting the hot water wash away the stress of it all, but the persistent throbbing of his ankle, combined with exhaustion, had him washing sketchily and drying himself even more sketchily. His fatigue was so vast, so weighty, that he experienced it as an entity, a huge, powerful animal pushing against him, forcing him to its will. He dragged on his pyjamas, muttering as the fabric clung to his damp legs, and staggered to his room, not even bothering to pull down the bedspread, but collapsing on top of it and letting the dark animal drag him down to its lair.

He panicked when he woke, looking frantically around the dim room for Binky, before the night's events trickled back, and he remembered that he didn't have to worry about Binky, ever again. The knowledge, instead of elating, depressed him. Binky would be well on his way home now. He wondered how long it would take them to get back. He should have asked when he had the chance. So many things he ought to have asked, and now he shook his head in irritation at himself. Alien beings from another planet, and he hadn't even found out if they had faster-than-light travel, or really anything.

Something roared past the house, and it came to him that this was what had woken him, the sound of some heavy vehicle going past. Anxiety clutched at his stomach, and he hurried on his clothes. The ones he'd been wearing were filthy, so he put on the ones he'd worn the day he came to the cottage. It seemed like years ago.

CHAPTER TWENTY-ONE

He found Mrs Butler in the kitchen, stirring something in a big pot. She turned, smiling, as he came in.

'Ah, Peter. Feeling better?'

'Much better, thanks. That smells good.'

'It's a bit of a mishmash, actually. I'm running low on food, so I'm making what my mother used to call Garbage Pie. We'll have to go shopping tomorrow.' She shook in spices from several different jars, apparently at random.

Peter frowned. 'How can we go shopping? They won't let us out.'

Mrs Butler chuckled. 'There's been a lot happening while you were sleeping. All that racket outside, that's Soldier Boy packing up and leaving.' A happy, secret smile wreathed her face, and she hummed a little tune as she crossed to the refrigerator. Tap, tap, tap. She was back in her high heels. All was right with the world.

All the same, he nearly jumped out of his skin when the doorbell rang. Mrs Butler, though, didn't even look around from rinsing her salad leaves.

'Get that, would you, Peter?'

'But – what if it's *them*?' It could hardly be anyone *but* them, he thought fuzzily. He was still a bit groggy from his long sleep, but something was wrong here. For the first time, he noticed that the windows were open, the curtains drawn back to catch any hint of breeze.

'It's not *them*. It's Mr Bamford. Go and let him in, give him a glass of sherry. In the cut-glass decanter on the drinks cabinet, the pink one. The glasses are underneath.'

It was indeed Mr Bamford, looking startlingly casual in a linen suit with an open-necked shirt. Peter caught a glimpse of dark hair at the 'V' of his shirt, and wondered uneasily whether his theft of the bottle of Raven Oil had been discovered. Everything else, he thought, could be explained away by fear of Kane and his men, but there was no excuse that he could think of for taking the Raven Oil, or, come to think of it, for being in Bamford's private quarters at all.

Just know nothing about it, and stick to that, he admonished himself. They can't prove anything. Just deny everything. You ran away because Kane threatened to burn you with a cigarette, and then you heard the soldiers letting off guns. They'd pointed their guns at the car, too, when they'd tried to leave. That was enough of an excuse for running away, and that was what he'd stick to. With luck, Old Farty would just think he'd finished the bottle anyway. And if he didn't, well, there were all those soldiers conveniently placed to take the blame.

Not that it mattered, he thought miserably as he poured from the pink decanter. He was sure to be expelled for running away, for stealing the bottle of vodka, and probably for other stuff he hadn't thought of yet. His hand trembled ever so slightly as he poured.

'Thank you, my boy,' said Mr Bamford, meeting him halfway and taking the glass. 'Next time, don't fill it so full. You should never fill a glass right up to the top, you know. It isn't done.'

'Sorry, sir,' said Peter, who knew this perfectly well. 'My hand slipped.'

'Barty, hello!' said Mrs Butler, coming in. 'You would not believe how good it is to see you.'

'Ah, hmm. Routing the forces of evil, eh?

Well, they've gone now. That Kane chap didn't reckon with the Old Boys' network, ah, hmmph. Biffy McLean's chief of his department. Head Boy here in '98. Rang him up and gave him hell. The army, too. Had their colonel here in '87, smarmy little blighter he was, too, remember him well. Sucked up to the masters and bullied the younger boys. Rang him up, end of problem. Left the school in the devil of a mess, though. Everything out of every cupboard, it looks like, and strewn all over the floors. All the locks broken open on the staff quarters. We'll have to get a locksmith in before term starts; carpenter too, I shouldn't wonder. You'll see to that, will you, Wendy?'

'Consider it done, Barty.' Mrs Butler poured sherry for herself, and perched on the arm of the sofa. 'I'll need to get back to the kitchen in a minute. I'm afraid dinner won't be anything too special.'

'I'm sure it will be up to your usual standards. *Nil desperandum*, eh?' He raised his glass in a toast. 'What's that you're drinking, Wendy? Sherry? Thought you were a vodka girl.'

'Ran out during the occupation. Oh, and that reminds me, Barty,' she took a sip, or rather more than a sip; she had knocked back half the glass, Peter saw. 'Peter,' she began. Peter, lurking by the door, felt the blood drain from his face. He'd never known what it meant in books when people's knees turned to water, but he did now. Here it came.

'Peter,' said Mrs Butler, 'has been such a tower of strength to me through it all. I don't know what I'd have done without him. So brave, and so helpful. I was really glad to have him here. I'd have gone out of my mind on my own.'

Dinner was a cheerful meal. The forbidding Mr Bamford, after three sherries and half a bottle of Cabernet, became quite jovial, and made a number of jokes in Latin, which nobody got. Mrs Butler recounted her skirmishes with Kane, and Peter, relaxing once it became apparent that for some reason Mrs Butler was not going to say anything about his misdeeds, filled in the details of what had happened in the Head's study before she had arrived.

'Good God,' bellowed Mr Bamford, turning quite purple. 'I'll be having another word with his Chief in the morning. Threatening a young boy like that. Disgraceful. He'll be out on his ear, just you see if he's not!'

'Go get 'em, Tiger!' said Mrs Butler. 'What was it all about, anyway, did they tell you?'

'Biffy told me some rubbish about a UFO sighting. Pack of nonsense. Been watching too much tabloid television, if you ask me.'

Peter choked, and took a hasty sip of water. Across the table, Mrs Butler caught his eye, looked hard at him and gave a tiny shake of her head. He stared back, eyes wide, giving her his best Face of Innocence, while behind it, his brain raced. What did she know?

As the meal continued, with escalating hilarity from the adults, now on their second bottle, he started to relax. Much of their talk was gossip about people they both knew, and he didn't, which left him free to turn things over in his mind, and it came to him that it didn't really matter what came out now; Binky was well away, and could not be got at. He cheered up enough to accept a second helping of the treacle pudding Mrs Butler had produced. It was rather better than the one they got at school dinners.

He had expected to be packed off to bed soon after the meal was over, but no one said anything about it, and at a quarter to twelve, almost unable to keep his eyes open, he stood up.

'I'd best be off to bed. Goodnight, Mrs Butler. Goodnight, Sir.'

'What? Don't be silly, Peter. It's New Year, I think you could stay up this once. Don't you stay up for New Year at home? It is the holidays, after all. He should definitely stay up, shouldn't he, Barty?'

Peter had never stayed up to see in the New Year. Aunty Jean, with whom he had until recently spent most of his time when not at school, had been an early riser, and thought staying up to see in the New Year was silly. The few times he'd been with his parents for it, there had always been some embassy function that he was considered too young to attend. He didn't like to say so, though, with Mrs Butler flushed with happiness and getting out a bottle of champagne and was it – yes, *three* glasses!

'It's almost time! Barty, I think Peter could have a glass with us, just this once, don't you?'

And the strict, stern headmaster of Tarrington Boys' Grammar beamed benevolently and waved a permissive hand. Peter pinched himself under the table, but yes, he was definitely awake.

He didn't like the champagne much, he found. It had the same sickly undertaste that the vodka bottle had given the water. But he finished the glass manfully, declining a refill in favour of another ginger ale.

It wasn't until Mr Bamford had departed, somewhat unsteadily, to walk back to the school that the subject came up.

'Help me clear, will you, Peter? You're not too tired, are you?'

He was, rather, but could hardly say so. As they stacked plates and gathered cutlery, Mrs Butler spoke, quite casually, without looking at him.

'I didn't want you to say anything in front of Mr Bamford. The thing is, you see, I know they've gone, and you probably think they're quite safe now, and you're probably right. But *you're* not safe, Peter.'

He froze in shock, a pile of plates held before him as if to ward off attack.

'Look, leave that for a minute, come and sit down. You have to understand this, because your life is going to depend on it.'

Peter set the stack of plates back on the table and followed her to the sofa. He felt very tired, the kind of tiredness that happens at the end of a huge task, when one is aching for rest, and then finds there is still more to be done. It's not fair, he wanted to shout. I'm only twelve.

'People like Kane,' began Mrs Butler, 'aren't like us. Mr Bamford's pulled strings and got him to back off and leave you alone, for now. But Kane isn't going to forget. He's got the resources of a big, powerful department behind him, and there'll be a file on this, and files can be reopened, Peter. It's very, very important that you never, ever breathe a word about any of this, not now, not next year, not even when you're grown up. Don't give them an excuse to come after you, do you see what I'm saying? You keep your head down and don't draw their attention, you'll be alright, but if you start talking about those... about *them*... don't ever, Peter. Not to anyone.'

His mind raced in small circles. What did

she know, and how? When she said *them*, was she talking about Binky and his parents? Or something else? He had to find out. But did it really matter? Suppose she did somehow know about Binky. Then she already knew, so it would be safe to talk about it. But if she didn't, if she meant something else... his tired brain couldn't get around the problem.

'Them?' he said, fishing. 'Them who?'

'*Them*. The people in the ship, whoever they were. Aliens, I suppose. I didn't actually see them.'

'What ship?' he asked, grasping at the straw of every child's trouble-avoidance technique.

'Peter, I *saw* it. I was in the forest, looking for you. I saw the ship, it appeared out of nowhere, all gold and glowing, and you were standing in the light, you looked like you were waving at it, and you stood there waving and it lifted off, and it rose up through the trees and then it zoomed straight up, until I lost sight of it in the stars.'

She stopped, out of breath. Her face was flushed and her eyes glowed with excitement. Peter knew an instant of total sympathy. In this moment she was another kid, just like him, and in his recognition of their kinship he almost loved her. Then the implication slammed into him, and he wanted to howl with the unfairness of it. It was *his* secret, the most important secret he had ever had. Of all the secret bits of knowledge he had collected so zealously, and hoarded so lovingly, this was by far the greatest, and he knew it would not be surpassed in his life. And he had to share it. It wasn't fair!

For a long moment he wavered between love and resentment. He squirmed in his discomfort, wriggling into the sofa cushions, and against his thigh he felt the hard lump of the bracelet. The sapphire bracelet, pressed on him with such joyful enthusiasm by Binky, that day in the attic. A wash of affection rolled over him, and he smiled at the memory. He would always have that, all to himself. And Mrs Butler hadn't even seen Binky.

Peter came to a decision.

'Mrs Butler, Binky – that's one of the aliens – gave me this. I want you to have it.'

Mrs Butler took the bracelet, holding it up to the light. 'Peter, I couldn't take this. These are real sapphires, I'm sure they are, it's worth a fortune. I can't possibly take it. You should give it to your mother.'

Peter set his lips firmly. 'Mum wasn't the one in the forest. She didn't see the ship. She didn't tell lies to save me from getting into trouble, she didn't face off Kane. You did that stuff. You're the one who was there for me this Christmas. I want you to have it. Please take it.'

As she wavered, still holding the bracelet, he drew a breath and went on, before he could bottle out.

'Listen,' he began. 'I'll tell you everything

that happened. I was exploring and I saw this bookcase….'

THE END

൙NO SUCH THING൫

ᏒᎧPART I ᏆᏯ

Callie Jones was parentified. She had it on good authority.

"Your trouble, Callie," said the school counsellor, "is that you're parentified." She said it with an air of smugness, as if she'd invented cyanide or something. Callie tried to paste the required expression on her face. Slightly worried but respectful, that should do it. She crossed her eyes slightly, her private act of defiance. It was Callie-speak for the raised middle finger.

Callie knew what her trouble was. It wasn't

being parentified, whatever that meant. It was being skinny, and flat as a board, and having dead white skin covered in freckles, like a Dalmatian. It was having a great bush of orange hair, like Ronald McDonald. It was also being top of the class in everything except gym. Being called Calliope wasn't much help, either. Thanks, Dad.

The counsellor was still rabbiting on, with her bullshit about parentification. Was that even a word? Callie let her mind drift. It had been last year that everything had suddenly gone all wrong. Callie had been happy enough in primary school. She'd had friends, and been good at everything, and had actually been quite popular. Then they'd moved here and she'd started high school, and everything had changed horribly. All of a sudden she had been surrounded by girls who were blonde, and tanned, and developing curves, and came up to about her shoulder. All of a sudden, Callie had become the class freak. Was she intrinsically a freak? Would it have happened just the same if she'd been able to stay at St Martha's? If the divorce hadn't happened, and they'd still had the big house with the pool, and she hadn't had to go to the state school? Were people at a private school kinder, more accepting, than state school kids? Was it, perhaps, a geographical anomaly? Was there something about Summer Bay that made people shitty? Or just the school? Callie toyed for a few moments with the idea of the school being positioned over a hellmouth, and rejected it. There was, after all, no such thing as a hellmouth.

Ms Clements, a.k.a. Ms Bullshit, was winding up her spiel. Some crap about the precious moments of childhood. What did she think would happen if Callie didn't cook, and clean, and do laundry? They'd be knee deep in rubbish and living on pizza and instant noodles, that was what. It was no use expecting Dad to be practical. Callie had realised that within a week of their move to Summer Bay. As soon as he'd got his computer set up, he'd been away Being A Writer, just as if nothing had changed. The only reason the old house had been nice was that Mum had had a cleaning lady three times a week and gardeners and a man to do the pool. Gradually, Callie had learned to take care of things. And she was doing just fine, thank you, Ms Parentified Bullshit. If only the bullies would leave her alone.

The counsellor was an idiot, Callie reflected on the ride home. She knew one thing about Callie, that her parents were divorced, and she let that dominate her thinking so that she couldn't see what was in front of her nose. Callie actually hadn't cared much when Mum had left. It had actually been more of a relief than anything, not to hear the fighting going on all the time. And they'd moved into the holiday house, out on the point. Callie loved the shabby old house. She loved its position, on the cliff looking out to sea. She loved the long bike ride to and from school. She loved that there weren't any neighbours closer than half a mile. She loved getting up in the early morning and climbing down the little track to the beach. If it weren't for Debbie Pearson and her gang, life would be just about perfect.

Dad was sitting at the kitchen table when she let herself in at the back door. Callie dropped her backpack in the corner and went to the fridge.

"What's up, Dad? Stuck with your book again?" It was a frequent occurrence.

Dad didn't reply. Turning, Callie noticed he looked oddly different. Sort of smaller, and old. When had he got old? Dad wasn't old. Forty was the new thirty, that was what it had said on the card she'd got him for his birthday last year.

"Dad? What's going on?"

He didn't answer; just kept on staring at some letter. Callie had no patience with drama. She snatched the paper out of his hand. Dear Mr Jones, she read. We note with concern that your monthly payments for March and April have not been received. This letter is a formal notification that you are in default of your obligation to make payments on your home loan, account number 998365-2345987. We regret to inform you that unless your account is brought into order by close of business on 29 May 2015, we shall have no option but to foreclose upon your home, and exercise our power of mortgagee sale pursuant to clause 51.3 of the loan agreement.

"Dad? What is this? What's a power of mortgagee sale? Is it bad?"

But he didn't say anything. Just buried his face in his hands and sat there shaking. Callie patted his shoulder and took the letter away to her room.

After two hours of googling, Callie knew quite a lot about how mortgages worked and what the results could be if you didn't keep up the payments. In NBL (non-bullshit language in the Callie Jones secret lexicon), either Dad coughed up the cash by five o'clock on 29 May, just over two weeks away, or else they would be out on the street. Or, even worse, Dad would be out on the street by himself and she'd be on her way to live with Mum and the car salesman she was shacking up with. That was too horrible to contemplate; Wayne, the salesman, was not only a home-wrecking moron (HWM), but on Callie's mandatory bi-monthly access weekends, was always making sleazy remarks and blocking doorways so that she was forced to squeeze past him. He'd even pinched Callie's bum a couple of times. Callie had complained to her mother, but had not been believed. She was Acting Out, her mother had said, whatever that meant. Callie suspected that, if translated into NBL, it would either mean she had said something an adult didn't want to hear, or would perhaps become mere empty noise, a sort of spoken carrier wave with no signal.

All through making dinner, and sitting through a silent, miserable meal, where Dad poked at his food and hardly ate anything, and the washing up, and the evening news, Callie worried away at the problem, turning it around to every side, chewing at it like a dog with a bone, but by the time she went up to her room, using as excuse for her unusually early retirement a history assignment she'd actually tossed off in the library at lunchtime, no solution had presented itself.

At daybreak, Callie climbed down the steep little track to the empty beach. She sat in her special place, a sandy cave just above the high water line, wrapped her arms around her legs, propped her chin on her knees, stared out to sea and gave herself up to random thought. All her best ideas came to her in this way; she didn't know if it was the place, or the attitude, or the time of day, but it was a frequent resort whenever she needed to think anything out. Just so had she sat when she'd come up with the idea for her costume for Cassandra Baldacci's fancy dress party, which everyone had said had been the best costume ever. Just so, when at eight years old she'd realised, after months of trying and trying, that she was never going to be good enough for her mother, so there was no point worrying about her any more. At that time, Callie's mother had been relegated to the class of People Who Didn't Matter, saving Callie from much unhappiness. She had been in this cave, she remembered, when she'd finally got the hang of quadratic equations. There was something magical about the cave, Callie felt: a feeling of total rightness that somehow acted to free her mind to do its best thinking.

No solution presented itself this time, though. She went over and over the elements of the situation: the mortgage, Dad's uncertain income, her own inability to get a job after school because they lived so far out of town. Not that Dad would have let her anyway, he'd completely freaked the one time she'd mentioned the possibility, and anyway, how much could a twelve-year-old kid earn? Not enough for the mortgage, that was for sure.

Unwillingly, Callie pictured the likely future. They'd lose the beach house, and then Dad would be homeless, she supposed he'd rent something, but she bet she'd get packed off back to Mum and Sleazy Wayne. The thought was unbearable, and for the first time in more than two years Callie, the capable one, found herself completely at a loss. Slowly, awkwardly, Callie began to cry.

What began with a faint snivelling quickly gained momentum, and within a few minutes Callie was letting it all out, sobbing and howling, torn by terrible grief for the life she loved and was to lose, yet at the same time experiencing an odd comfort as she truly let go for the first time in years. Forgotten was the running list that usually sat tucked in a corner at the front of her mind - Dad's breakfast, the washing that should be hung out before she left for school, the gutters that needed clearing out before the weekend's forecast heavy rain. Callie threw herself down on the sandy floor and gave way to sorrow.

She never knew how much time passed before the voice recalled her to herself. It was a small voice, tiny, faint and far away, but unmistakably real in its querulous irritation.

"I say, there. Aren't you ever going to shut up? Some of us would like to get some sleep, you know."

Callie hiccupped in surprise and caught her breath on a sob. She froze, listening. But there was only the sound of waves beating on the shore, and the far-off cry of a seagull.

"That's better. It's never any use bellowing about things. It doesn't do any good, and it annoys people."

Callie sat up, forgotten tears drying on her

face. "What - who is that?"

"What a question! It's me, of course. Or rather, it is I. Who else?"

Callie looked around the apparently empty cave. "Are you invisible?" This couldn't be happening. Invisible people didn't exist, just like fairies and all the rest of that crap. Callie had shut the lid on her imagination years before, when she'd first become aware of what the world was really like. Her mother couldn't be relied on for anything, and with her father being the way he was, her little family couldn't afford a second dreamer. She must be hallucinating, she thought. Perhaps she was getting ill. A wave of panic swept through her. She couldn't be ill, not now.

The tiny voice continued, rasping irascibly. "Up here, to your left."

Callie turned slowly, wondering. The cave was completely empty. Hold on, though, it wasn't; she'd caught a glimpse of movement, halfway up the rock wall. She moved closer, peering intently, and all in a moment light and shade resolved and, with a gasp of shock and wonder, she realised what she was seeing.

The tiny dragon clung to a slight unevenness in the rock, golden wings waving, half-unfurled to catch the reflected glint of the rising sun. No wonder she hadn't seen it, Callie thought; the whole creature would have fitted into a matchbox with room to spare. She bent closer. It was perfect, a creature of story, gold scales glistening and the wings like tissue.

"Back off, girl, don't BREATHE on me. Young people today. Really!"

"Sorry." Callie apologised from habit, the ingrained habit of years that kept all her rudenesses tiny and subtle and codified. "Um, my name's Callie, Callie Jones."

"Know, then, Callie Jones, that you are speaking with the great Maelogan."

"How do you do, Mrs Logan." The polite

formula rose automatically to Callie's lips. She felt dizzy. She must be dreaming, that was it. Presently she'd wake up in her bed, and none of this would have happened. She'd go downstairs and start breakfast for Dad, and if she was very, very lucky, that about the mortgage would also have been part of the dream.

"Mrs Logan? MRS LOGAN? Be thou taking the piss, thou rascally urchin?"

"Um, no, sorry, wasn't that what you said?"

"I said MAELOGAN."

Callie was confused. "Should I call you May, then? Or Miss Logan?"

"Foolish child. Maelogan is an ancient Welsh name, meaning Divine Prince. You dishonour me with your stupidity. You disgrace yourself. In my day...."

"I'm really very sorry," put in Callie quickly. "I didn't mean any harm. We don't come much in the way of Welsh names, you know."

"See that you remember it, then. I didn't come all the way to this godforsaken place to have my ancient name mangled by whippersnappers."

"No, sir." Clearly extreme respect was the way to go. As, indeed, it generally seemed to be with very small humans, Callie thought, remembering the explosive temper and paranoid sensitivity of Miss McCorkerdale, the tiny games mistress at St Martha's.

"Well, just see that you remember. Now, what was all that crying about? Hey? Come on, girl, I haven't got all day."

Callie wondered what to say. A dragon, a creature of myth and legend, couldn't be expected to understand about mortgages, she thought, and so indeed it was. By the time she'd explained what one was, and why Dad had to have one (why does he not go forth and take his land by conquest?) she'd had to cover most of the basic political and economic structure of today's Australia, rather like sitting a Social Studies exam, and was feeling quite exhausted.

The dragon, or Maelogan, as she must remember to call him, sat silent for a while, waving his wings gently. A tiny wisp of steam wafted from his nose.

"But why," said Callie, "I mean, I thought dragons were mythical. Magic creatures, not real."

Maelogan snorted. "We're real enough. Magic, too. Does it have to be one or the other? Stupid girl."

"Well, yes, it does rather, as there's no such thing as magic."

"No such thing? No such THING? I'll show you no such thing. Stupid girl. Lacking respect for your betters." He subsided into a muttering grumble, in which the words 'stupid' and 'no respect' could occasionally be distinguished.

"Well go on, then, do some magic."

"Do some magic. Do some magic. Do you think I'm a performing animal, girl, to do tricks for your amusement? I ought to fry you where you sit. Be off with you, now."

"Off? This is MY cave. I've been coming here for years. Why don't you bugger off back to where you came from, hang out with all the other stupid dragons. Which, by the way, don't exist," Callie added with what was for her a staggering lack of logic, but she'd lost her temper. "Anyway, I have to go, I'll be late for school."

As she turned to exit the tiny cave, the dragon called after her. She almost ignored him, but there was something about the tiny cry, ending on something that was almost, but not quite, a sob. It was the sound of desperate need, and Callie, who'd been there herself, could not quite bring herself to ignore it.

"Wait, don't go... please," said the dragon. The last word appeared to give him some trouble. Callie paused in the mouth of the cave, not wanting to deny the appeal, but still cross.

"It's been so long, you see," said Maelogan. "I haven't spoken to another sentient creature for, oh, hundreds of years. Hundreds and hundreds, and I'm so lonely... and I'm shrinking, look at me, soon there won't be anything left of me."

"What do you mean, shrinking? People don't shrink. They either grow or they stop, not shrink."

"Your sort of people, perhaps, but my people, dragons, are different. You see, we are magic, at least partly, and we require certain things. Not just food and water and so on, like you gross beings."

"What? Who are you calling gross?"

"It just means the opposite of magical. You see, Callie Jones, a magical or partly-magical creature such as a dragon also requires intangible sustenance."

"Like what?"

"Well, it's complicated, but to put it simply in a way your limited human mind can grasp, we require belief."

"What, you need something to believe in?"

"No, stupid girl. We need someone to believe in US. You don't think we were always as small as I am now, do you?"

Callie thought of St George and the Dragon. Certainly the dragons of legend were huge, otherwise they could hardly have carried off maidens. And St George could have just stepped on his dragon and squashed it, instead of rushing about poking it with a lance, or whatever.

"Okay, so, what, you mean you all shrank because people stopped believing in you?"

"Well, yes, basically. Of course, there was more to it than that, a lot more, but in simple terms that you can understand, yes, that's pretty well what happened. A lot of us have died, perhaps all of us, I haven't seen another dragon for more than eight hundred years myself, although there were rumours a while back, but that was on the other side of the world anyway."

Callie digested this for a minute, fitting it into what she knew about the world, not distinguishing between the everyday and the startlingly new, because it was all observed fact.

"So if you shrank because people didn't believe in you, will you grow again if they do?"

"Who knows? I think I feel a little stronger. Do you think you could bring me something to eat?"

"Sure. When I come back after school, but I have to go now, or I'll be late."

The dragon's wings flapped, conveying an impression of agitation. "When will you return?"

"This afternoon. I get back about four, so I'll come down then, okay?" The agitated flapping didn't diminish. "Um, before sunset. Will that do?"

"You will return? You won't forget?"

What planet was he on, Callie wondered. Seeing a dragon, a real dragon, even if it was tiny, discovering that there were dragons, did he think she was going to forget all about it, as she might forget her gym tunic? Still, she supposed that to him, dragons were ordinary, just as to her, being a freak was ordinary.

"Don't start snivelling again, girl," snapped the dragon.

All through Maths, and Double Geography, and lunchtime, when as usual she hid in the library to avoid Debbie Pearson and her nasty gang, Callie's mind whirled with wonder. When Debbie sat behind her in English and constantly poked her in the back with her ruler, she hardly noticed, other than to shift her chair forward. Getting on her bike to come home, she felt the sore places on her ribs and for a moment didn't even know what they were. In History, she was told off for staring out the window and not paying attention, a thing that never happened.

The ride home was taken in a fury of speed that covered the five miles in record time, and it was barely four by the time Callie, hastily changed into jeans and a t-shirt, her school uniform most uncharacteristically left in a tangled heap on her bedroom floor, was sliding down the track to the beach, clutching in one hand a rather spotty banana and in the other a can of sardines.

She saw the dragon at once. He was crouched at the cave's entrance, and in the afternoon sun he seemed almost to glow from within. Callie's heart gave a little skip. He was hers, only hers, no one else knew about him. More precious to Callie than a supposedly mythical being turning out to be real was the thought of perhaps having a friend again.

"Here I am! I brought you some food. Sardines and a banana, I hope that's alright." She tugged the ring pull and ripped the can open. "They're ones in spring water."

The dragon approached the can and sniffed dubiously at its contents. "Fish, is it? Well, I suppose it's better than nothing. And what's that other thing?"

"A banana," Callie repeated, peeling it for him and laying it beside the sardines.

"Oh, one of THOSE." He shuddered delicately. "Those things are the reason I ended up in this godsforsaken place. Went to sleep in a tree, and next thing I was stuck in a ship's hold for a fortnight. Nothing to eat there except rats and a few spiders. Those big tarantulas. Longest two weeks I ever spent." He turned from the banana and took a cautious bite of sardine.

"You ate a tarantula?"

"Yes, of course, it was that or a solid diet of rat. They weren't so bad. Crunchy, but no flavour to speak of."

"Couldn't you have eaten the bananas?"

"Not much value in fruit, not for my kind. We generally eat only meat. This isn't bad, though. A bit oily. Bring some red meat next time."

Next time, Callie thought, hugging her secret knowledge to herself.

"While I'm eating, you can tell me why you were crying like that this morning. Unless it was some kind of devotional exercise? If it was, I don't want to hear about it. Heard enough about you humans' stupid religions in the Crusades."

"You were in the Crusades?" Callie's eyes lit up. Imagine hearing about it all first hand. History was her favourite subject.

"Yes, yes, never mind that. Come now, what was all that weeping about? Tell me about it, you'll feel better."

The bank's letter, forgotten in the

excitement of the day, slammed back into Callie's stomach with a jolt of hot guilt and fear.

"I told you this morning, about the mortgage and that. Don't you remember?"

The dragon snorted, spraying flecks of sardine. "Of course I remember, but why cry about it? They can have this mordee, whatever you called it, thing, I don't see why that should bother you."

Callie sighed. "Because they'll take our home. They can, you see. And we'll lose this place, and everything...."

"Alright," mumbled the dragon rather indistinctly. He swallowed and lifted his head to stare at her with emerald eyes. "What will stop them?"

"Well, money, I suppose. I mean, if we paid all the arrears right away, I guess everything would go back to normal. But that's the thing, Mae, we haven't got the money. We haven't got any money. Dad's a writer, you see."

"A writer? What's that? Something like a pauper?"

Callie sniggered in spite of herself. It was something like, she thought. "He writes books, and when he sells one, money comes in, and there's a trickle of royalties, but they only get paid every quarter, and he sort of ekes things out in between. Basically, the big payment comes when he sells a new book, and that hasn't been for a while now, he's stuck again with the one he's writing."

"A scholar!" Maelogan's voice took on a new tone of respect.

"Well, kind of. He writes detective books."

"What's a detective?"

"It's a person who - oh, never mind. The thing is, we've got to get hold of a shitload of money before the 29th of May. And I can't see any way we can do it."

"And conquest is really out of the

question?" asked Maelogan wistfully. "It's really the best way, you know. Simple and clean and honest. You know where you are with Fort Mayne."

"Well, we don't do things that way in Australia. Get over it. It's got to be money."

Apparently sated, Maelogan backed away from the sardines and curled up on the sandy floor in a patch of sunlight. He began to wash his face, for all the world like a tiny cat, Callie thought. After a few minutes, he spoke again.

"Well, of course, that's fairly easy. Oh yes, easy to fix if it's just gold you want." His voice seemed to gain confidence. "I could do that for you. There would be a price, of course."

"A price? What sort of a price? Do you mean like my first-born child or something?"

Maelogan snorted. "Don't be ridiculous, child. What would I want with a squalling baby? You've been listening to too many fairy tales."

"Well, what, then? What is it you want, I'll get it for you if I can." If it's legal, Callie silently cautioned herself. And not too evil.

"It's not what I want. It's not a matter of trade." Maelogan's voice dripped with the scorn of commerce that can only be truly felt by one who has never worked in his life. "It's the magic. Magic always demands a price. Don't you know anything?"

"Magic," Callie scoffed. "There's no such thing as magic."

"Well, call it something else, then. Call it... a miracle. Is that easier for you?"

"There's no such thing as miracles," Callie countered. She'd stopped believing in God when her parents had split up. It had coincided with her sixth grade teacher being some kind of religious nut who was always carrying on about God and making them stay inside and have prayer meetings at playtime. The combination had been too much, and Callie had gone right off the whole business. "Anyway, even if there were, miracles are religious. They only come from God."

"Whatever," sighed Maelogan, sounding for all the world like a spoiled teenager. He seemed to have a very modern vocabulary for someone who'd been out of touch for eight hundred years. You'd have thought he'd be all thee and thou, Callie thought. "I can fix this for you, but there will be a price, and it might not be a price you want to pay. Do you understand, child?"

"No, not really. If you're the one doing it, why don't you know what the price will be?"

"Because I'm not the one demanding it, don't you see? It's not a price such as, give me this sheep and I give you six groats. It's a thing of nature. It's balance. It's like, oh, suppose you want to eat five bushels of peaches, well the price will be a sick stomach, do you see? And there's no bargaining with that, it can't be altered."

"So what, you just mean consequences?"

"Not exactly. It's more than just that. But that's the nearest I can come to it."

"I don't care. Nothing could be worse than losing this place."

"So, you ask my help?" Maelogan's voice had taken on a deep and portentous tone.

Callie threw caution to the winds. "Yes. If you can help us, then please help us. I'll do anything, anything that's not wrong, that is," she amended.

"Very well. Near your house is a bush with red flowers. Dig under it, to a depth of half a man's height, and you will find the solution to your problem."

"What bush? We haven't got any flowers in our garden, I'm crap at gardening and so is Dad."

"Near your house," Maelogan repeated,

"there will be a bush with red flowers. Dig under it to the depth of half a man's height, and you will find your answer. Do not argue with me, child. But remember, there will be a price, and once you accept my help, there is no evading it."

Callie sighed. It was just more bullshit. There wasn't any bush with red flowers, she knew that for sure. For a moment she'd thought... but there, dragons were real, obviously, and so were no doubt just as full of bullshit as most humans. She looked at her watch. It was nearly six; she needed to get back and start dinner.

"I have to go now. Do you want that banana or not?"

"Not. But you can leave the fish. Tomorrow, bring me some meat."

"Geez, don't bother asking nicely or anything, will you?"

"Your pardon, Mistress Calliope. I prithee, of thy great charity, that thou shouldst bless this humble creature with a good beefsteak on the morrow." Maelogan's voice dripped with bitter sarcasm.

"Alright, alright, just kidding, relax, I'll bring you something tomorrow after school." She gathered up the now rather brown and slimy banana and its skin. She'd toss it on the beach for the seagulls. Callie hated waste.

It was almost dark by the time she reached the top of the cliff, and there was no time to be lost searching the yard for nonexistent flowers. Callie hurried inside to get dinner started. After the dishes were done, and the meat off a forequarter chop (sequestered from Callie's own dinner and substituted with extra mashed potatoes) squirrelled away in foil at the back of the refrigerator to be taken to Maelogan tomorrow, she went upstairs to do her homework. She usually did the bulk of it in the library at lunchtime, but she'd been so preoccupied that day thinking about dragons that nothing had been accomplished.

She was up until after eleven finishing her algebra, focussing relentlessly on each problem, refusing to let her mind wander to the cave on the beach. There's been too much silly daydreaming today, she scolded herself. Alright, so dragons are real after all, that's no reason to fail your exams. It was looking as though Callie would have to rely on the slim chance of a scholarship if she wanted to go to university, and you couldn't start too early, she knew. This year's results would determine her placement in next year's subject streams, and if she got relegated to a mere Credit level stream in any subject it would be very hard to get back into Advanced, if it was even possible, and there would go her hopes of getting into Medicine.

After her late night, Callie overslept, and had to rush out the door without breakfast, leaving Dad to look after himself. There was no time to visit the beach cave, and certainly no time to swan about the garden looking for nonexistent flowers. By the time she'd made it to the other end of a gruelling Wednesday, which started with double Maths and ended with sport afternoon, Callie's personal hell, where she had to endure two hours of surreptitious bashing by Debbie Pearson and her horrible friends on the basketball court, Callie was exhausted, shaking, and covered with bruises. Sadly she unlocked her bicycle and started to pump up the tyres, which had been let down again.

By the time she reached home, Callie was almost weeping with tiredness. She wheeled her bicycle into the garage and went to let herself in the back door. But before she reached the back porch, Callie had frozen in her tracks, tiredness forgotten, dropping her backpack on the ground with small regard for its precious cargo of textbooks, and stood staring in amazement at the ratty, rangy old geranium by the back steps, now a mass of scarlet blooms.

Her first thought was to rush inside to tell Dad, but she checked it before she'd taken more than a single step. What could she tell him, after all? That the moribund bush had suddenly decided to flower? He wouldn't thank her for interrupting his work to hear that, and he certainly wouldn't understand why it must be instantly dug up. She'd better just dig it up herself, and not say anything.

Tiredness and bruises forgotten, she raced back to the garage for the rusty tools.

Digging the hole was harder than it looked, and within the hour Callie's hands were blistered and sore, and her back screamed for relief. She'd only been actually excavating for about half that time, too, as the first half hour had been occupied with carefully digging round the geranium to save as much of its root ball as possible, so that it could be replanted afterwards. In the two years since her parents' separation, Callie had grown deeply enamoured of thrift, and even with the prospect of saving their house, she saw no reason to destroy the only pretty thing the garden had ever produced. Geraniums were tough, she knew; in primary school they'd done a project where they'd started little ones just by putting cut pieces into jars of water and leaving them on the windowsill. Nearly all of them had grown roots and lived. She'd put the geranium in a bucket of water; hopefully that would keep it alive for a while.

She was only about a foot down when she remembered her promise, and the chop she'd saved for Maelogan. Well, that would be an excuse for a little break from the digging. She'd take it down to him, and then when she got back she'd find those mittens she'd had that time they'd gone for a snow holiday. They'd be too small now, but surely they'd be enough to give her hands a bit of protection. She didn't need to worry about wrecking them, she knew; there would be no more holidays to the snow, or anywhere else that cost money.

Money, she reflected as she slipped and slid down the track to the beach, almost losing her feet in her haste. It changed everything. For the first time, she wondered how much her new freak status might have to do with no longer getting dropped off in a late-model BMW, and her third-hand school uniforms from the op shop. You could see the faded marks where her tunic had been let down, and the material of her shirts was worn thin. Could these things have more to do with her freakdom than her own appearance? Callie had never given much thought to money before. They'd been rich and now they were poor, but the change hadn't really had much of an impact on her, other than the all-good one of living here with just Dad. Callie didn't miss her mother at all, having given up on her long before the split. She was just happy not to have to listen to the fights.

Maelogan was waiting for her on his rock at the front of the cave. He was bigger than he'd been yesterday. Callie rubbed her eyes, but it was undeniable - since she'd left him, he'd more than doubled his size, and was now about as big as her clenched fist. He looked shinier than yesterday, too, and more solid, as if he'd filled out a little bit. He greeted her with enthusiasm, tearing into the chop as if he hadn't seen food for days. Callie watched as he ate, noticing how he held it, sitting up on his hindquarters and using his claws almost like hands. He was a beautiful thing, she thought, lovely in and of himself, with an elegance of form that reminded her rather of those tall thin dogs in pictures she'd seen of old tapestries.

Finally, he swallowed the last scrap of meat and sat licking grease off his whiskers, just like a cat, Callie thought. He did have whiskers, too, oddly enough; being a reptile, she'd thought that wouldn't be a thing. Better not ask, though. He might be sensitive about his appearance. Callie knew all too well what that was like.

"So, have you found it yet?" he asked, having completed his grooming.

"Found what?"

"The answer to your problems, of course. Have you not dug up the bush yet, the bush with the red flowers?"

"I've started. It's not as easy as it looks, digging, you know. Look at my hands." She held out her hands, with their crop of weeping blisters.

"Tut tut, you should be more careful. Never mind, I can fix that for you. Just hold your hands still. It might be best not to look."

"Not to look? Look at what? What are you doing?" For the little dragon was drawing in a deep, deep breath, swelling up almost like a frog. Callie knew a moment's misgiving, rapidly supplanted by sheer panic as Maelogan blew out a blast of blue flame, almost invisible in the sunlight.

She cried out as the flames enveloped her shaking hands, but before she could snatch them away, recoiling in horror, she realised that she wasn't burned, that the flames were oddly cool, that, in fact, it didn't hurt at all, and was really quite soothing, as if antiseptic cream were being softly spread on her blisters. As the flames died down and winked out, she saw with wonder that there was no trace of the blisters; the skin was perfectly new and clean, and tingling slightly, but definitely not painful, not at all.

"Wow," she said softly. "Far out."

Maelogan preened himself. "Yes, I haven't lost the old touch. There now, you should be able to finish the job before that wears off. The effect will last for three days, sunrise to sunset."

"Effect? What effect?"

"Well, it's a little protection for you. Nothing will be able to harm your hands until it wears off."

"Are you serious?"

"Of course. I told you we are creatures of magic." He seemed to feel that all that needed to be said had been said. "Well, what are you waiting for, girl? Go and get on with the job. It will only last until sunset of the third day, you know. And tomorrow, don't cook the meat so much. It spoils the flavour. Bring it raw, and I'll toast it myself, the way I like it."

What with school, and homework, and laundry, and visiting Maelogan with raw meat every afternoon, and seeing that Dad ate more or less regular meals, Callie was still digging as the sun slipped towards the horizon on Friday. Luckily, she'd had no awkward explaining to do, as Dad hadn't left the house for weeks, and seemed to be a fixture at his desk by the front window, which fortunately did not afford a view of the back of the house where her excavations were being carried on. It was lucky, too, that they hadn't any neighbours close enough to notice what she was up to and start asking awkward questions. But as the hole grew ever deeper and the pile of dirt grew ever larger, Callie grew ever less hopeful, and would have given up altogether, had it not been for the undeniable fact that, despite her furious efforts with shovel and mattock, which left her shaking with exhaustion every evening and stiff and sore every morning, her hands remained pristine and comfortable, the skin as soft and smooth as if she'd spent the time rubbing in hand lotion, not even dirt seeming to cling to them. If the one magic had worked, she told herself, there was no reason to give up on the other, at least until she had reached the specified depth, which she interpreted as being three feet. Although, she thought, hadn't people been rather small in the middle ages? Might it, perhaps, be only two feet, or two feet six?

She was up to her waist in the hole, though, as the sun sank below the horizon. Callie was a tall girl, and she knew her waist had to be well over three feet above the ground. Sadly she propped her tools against the side of the house, checked the water level in the bucket, where the geranium seemed to be thriving, and went inside to wash for dinner.

It rained late that night, a sudden, torrential rain, with wind that lashed the trees back and forth and thunder that barked at random intervals, startling Callie over and over again as she lay in bed until she was a mass of nervous irritation. Finally the storm abated, and she lay listening to the water running in the gutters, hoping Maelogan would be alright in his cave. Perhaps she ought to take him something to make a nest out of. She had a couple of old t-shirts she'd outgrown, that she'd been planning to cut up for cleaning rags. Those would do. She'd take them down in the morning. No school tomorrow, she remembered with dreamy pleasure. Two days free of Debbie Pearson and her crew. Two days of peace. Then she remembered the bank, and felt miserably guilty. She had wasted three days on that stupid hole, days in which she might have come up with a sensible plan to save the house, and she had nothing to show for it, nothing except a big stupid hole and a geranium that she'd probably killed.

Saturday dawned clear and bright, and Callie was up and dressed with the first rays of light. She loved the early mornings best of all. She loved the peace and quiet, the stillness, and the way the world always seemed clean, as if night had rinsed away the grime of yesterday.

The first thing she'd do, she decided, was fill in that stupid hole and replant the poor old geranium. Perhaps at least it could survive, to gladden the house's next occupants with its cheerful red flowers. Someone, at least, would get something out of it.

She opened the back door, snuffing in a deep, satisfying breath of morning air, and went to look at the hole. At some point during the storm it must have filled with water, because the bottom was all muddy and sloppy-looking. She'd better measure first how much to fill in before she put the geranium in.

Taking a rough measure of the depth of the bucket with her forearm, Callie kicked off her shoes and jumped into the hole, and collapsed screaming with pain as her foot came down on a sharp pointy something just below the surface of the muddy water.

Crumpled in the mud, Callie keened and clutched her foot, the pain like nothing she'd ever known. She couldn't even see. Hours passed, or a few minutes or seconds; Callie couldn't tell. All she knew was that she was submerged in a tide of red agony. As the first intensity of pain receded, Callie opened her eyes and, bracing herself, looked at the sole of her foot, at the white skin now disfigured by a huge, purple mark. Surprisingly, there was very little blood. A slight graze at the centre of the bruise oozed a few drops, but the ragged, gaping hole right through her foot that her mind's eye had conjured based on the more lurid crucifixion paintings was not to be seen.

Now that she wasn't worried about losing half her foot, Callie was able to think past the immediate pain to wonder what on earth had caused it. It had to be something buried in the dirt, she reasoned, and the rain had washed it into soup, so that when she'd jumped down, it had been sticking up below the surface of the mud. Curiously, she felt about in the sloppy bottom of the hole. It felt like metal, a jagged, irregular point of metal sticking up out of the mud. Could she bail out the hole, and get a better look at it?

Carefully, Callie climbed out of the hole and levered herself upright, leaning on the shovel. She cringed as she put weight on her injured foot, but the hurt part was in the arch, so she could more or less walk as long as she kept on the toes of that foot. She hoped she wouldn't need a doctor; that would be more expense they couldn't afford. Perhaps Maelogan would be able to heal it, as he'd done her hands?

In the kitchen, she grabbed the glass measuring jug. It held two cups, that should be big enough to get most of the sloppy mud out of the way. She made her slow and painful way back outside and knelt at the edge of the hole. She didn't bother trying to stay out of the mud; she was already covered in it from head to foot. She lay down on her stomach and reached down to scoop out cupfuls of mud.

It only took four or five scoops, and Callie could see the cause of her injury. Wow, no wonder it hurt, it was like a little mountain peak. Funny colour it was, not really like a rock at all. Intrigued, Callie scooped a little clean water from the long-suffering geranium's bucket and drizzled it over the protuberance.

And there in the morning light was revealed the unmistakable glint of gold.

ഇPART IIര

It hadn't taken all that much, Callie reflected as she packed up her books at the end of class. The bullies had melted away like morning mist once the tabloids picked up on the story. GIRL, TWELVE, FINDS BIGGEST NUGGET EVER IN BACK YARD. The massive chunk of gold had been worth almost a million dollars. Whether it had been Callie's newfound prosperity or her sudden fame, Pearson and her gang had backed right off. They'd even tried to be friendly, but Callie wasn't that much of a fool.

The bank had backed off too, once the story had hit the papers and Dad had gone to see them and gently explained what a good feature it would make for tabloid television if they foreclosed while he was still in the process of realising its value. Take all the time you need, they'd said. They'd even frozen the interest for the two months it had taken before Dad actually got his hands on the cash. Sad, really, Callie thought, how people changed so dramatically in the presence of a lot of money. Not surprising, but disappointing all the same. She wasn't all that keen on people these days, except for Dad, of course. She'd dreamed of being one of the popular girls, but now that she was pretty well the most popular girl in the school, all she wanted, she found, was to be left alone. Where had all those girls been when she'd been new in the school and needed a friend? They were all bullshit. Maelogan was all the friend she needed. She loved listening to his stories of the crusades, the great plague, and all the events of European history, even if half of it was, as she suspected, pure fiction. She loved his acerbic comments, and even his periodic grumpy moods. Maelogan was real, more real than any of the two-faced bitches that fawned around wanting her to go for coffee after school. Callie didn't like coffee all that much, but if she did want it, she'd make it herself, in the big flash espresso machine that had been Dad's first celebratory purchase after the mortgage was finally paid off. They owned their house free and clear now. They'd never have to worry again.

Thank God Dad hadn't got all silly about the money. Like her, he wasn't really all that interested in it. He'd been happy, of course, but apart from the espresso machine and a computer upgrade, he hadn't really done anything out of the ordinary. He'd offered to get Callie's room done up like in the magazines, but Callie liked her silvery grey scrubbed floorboards and faded chintz curtains just the way they were. She had consented to new school uniforms, though, and a few clothes. It was lovely to own things that no one had worn before, things that fit properly, and still had the crisp shine of newness the first time they were worn.

For a wonder, she hadn't let herself be too distracted by it all, either. Callie knew how sudden popularity went to people's heads, she'd seen *Mean Girls* five times, but it didn't really seem to have made any difference to her, probably, she thought, because her popularity had been too sudden to seem at all real, or anything but ridiculous. When Debbie Pearson had come up to her in the schoolyard, going that her hair was a totally awesome colour, and asking her to hang out after school, the day after the story had been on the six o'clock news, all Callie had wanted to do was laugh. She'd changed her habits not a whit, riding her bike home after school and hanging out with Maelogan, who had grown almost to the size of a small dog. As the weather had turned towards winter, he'd moved from the beach cave into her room, where he perched at night on the curtain rail, occasionally taking to the air to chase a moth and send it, scorched and sizzling, spiralling to the floor.

Callie made her way to the bike shed and unchained her bike. It was the same beat-up old one she'd had since they'd moved here. Dad had wanted to buy her a new one, but Callie treasured the old bike. It represented independence to her. She'd seen it from the window of the bus the first week she'd ridden to school on the rattly, smelly, once-a-day school bus, thrown out on the nature strip for the hard waste collection. She'd counted the minutes all day, and had gone straight there after school, missing the bus and walking the five miles home wheeling the decrepit thing. She had spent every spare moment on it for weeks, polishing and oiling and putting on new tyres bought with her carefully hoarded pocket money, until finally it was functional, and she could forget the bus and take herself to school and anywhere she wanted to go. Nothing could replace it.

The bike was, of course, unmolested. These

days, it always was. Callie smiled, thinking of all the times she'd had to pump up the tyres, or wipe something nasty off the seat, before starting the long ride home. That was all over now, it seemed.

She paused at the top of the last, tiring hill to look down at the house. There it was, home. Dad would be pounding away at his computer, muttering distractedly with his hair standing on end. Maelogan would probably be in the garden, chasing insects. She had worried when he'd first moved up from the cave. It frightened her to think of someone seeing him. That first fortnight after she'd found the nugget had been dreadful, with the phone ringing nonstop and strange, dodgy-looking men and overly made-up women prowling round their garden and sometimes trying to see in the windows. She had imagined busloads of scientists descending on them, capturing Maelogan and shutting him up in a cage, perhaps vivisecting him. Maelogan's blithe assurance that other people couldn't see his 'true nature' had reassured her not at all, since she hadn't believed it. Dragons really existing was one thing, but you were either visible or you weren't, and if you were visible, anyone could see that you were basically a big, winged lizard.

There was a car parked out the front of their house. A big, shiny one. Callie frowned. She hoped it wasn't more reporters. She kicked off and let the bike roll down the steep hill, enjoying the rush of speed, the wind in her ears blowing away the creeping cobwebs of doubt.

When she coasted to a stop at the front gate, flushed and exhilarated, the car was still there. It was a Mercedes, she now saw. Not reporters, then. But not anyone they knew, either. She shrugged out of her backpack and went inside.

There was no one in the kitchen, which wasn't all that surprising, Callie thought. A person in a flash car like that would rate the sitting room. She tossed her backpack in a corner and went to poke her nose in, curious who the visitor could be.

And then her world shattered.

"Callie, DAHLING! I've come HOME!"

Callie couldn't see, couldn't breathe, couldn't think. Her nose was pressed into a soft, squishy mound of cashmere-coated flesh, her neck caught in a stranglehold. Her nostrils burned with the fumes of a heavy, musky perfume. She wriggled frantically, trying to break free, to get a breath of unpolluted air.

The iron grip gave way suddenly, and she would have fallen if she hadn't been held by clawlike fingers gripping her upper arms.

"Let me LOOK at you! Oh, my little girl is growing up!"

Callie wanted to vomit. "Hello, Mum," she said. Her voice came out pale and sickly.

Mum continued to screech, mostly about

how she claimed to have missed Callie and Dad, and her great love for her family (a Mother's Heart, etc.) Callie watched her, reflexively crossing her eyes in the secret, Callie-speak gesture of rejection. Why'd you shack up with Wayne then, she wanted to ask. How come you forgot my birthday. Except for her court-ordered access weekends every two months, Callie had not seen or heard from her mother in the two years since the separation.

She glanced over at Dad, hunched at one end of the sofa. He would be no help. He was sitting frozen, a sickly smile on his face, and wouldn't meet her eyes. She could tell from the way he held his shoulders that he had the beginnings of one of his headaches.

Her mother finally let go. Callie rubbed her arms, wondering if she'd have bruises. Could she show them to the school counsellor and get her access visits stopped? It would be worth a try, if the bruises came up. Perhaps she could sort of help them along a bit. Her white, freckled skin did show bruises easily. For a moment, she allowed herself a little dream of never seeing her perfume-drenched, screeching mother again, but her practical nature reasserted itself.

"Are you staying for dinner?"

"Dinner!" screeched her mother. "I've come HOME, darling, home for always."

For the first time in her life, Callie fainted.

Fainting turned out not to be anything like what one saw on the movies. It was more, Callie reflected as she hunched miserably over the toilet, heaving and spitting, as if she had just been standing there and the floor had swung up and bopped her on the head. She'd woken up on the floor, with Dad sponging her face with the dish towel and her mother screeching away in a full-on hysterical drama queen attack, stomping about the room in her five-inch heels. Callie had had to snatch her hand quickly away from the descending spikes. Mum had sobbed and wailed while Dad helped her to the bathroom.

There seemed to be nothing left to come up, which was hardly surprising as Callie had, as usual, skipped lunch to spend her free hour in the school library, getting her homework out of the way. She flushed, rinsed her mouth and splashed cold water on her face. Time to face the music. Glancing at her watch, she noticed with surprise that less than ten minutes had elapsed since she'd arrived home.

She found her parents in the sitting room. Dad was back on the sofa, jammed into one end with a hand shielding his eyes. Her mother was next to him, clutching his arm and cooing. Callie noticed that despite all the sobbing and howling she'd been doing a few minutes ago, her mascara didn't seem to be smudged.

Dinner was a trial for everyone. Callie's mother looked aghast at the plain grilled chops, mashed potatoes and steamed green beans, and proceeded to push her food around the plate without eating anything. Dad appeared to have been turned into a zombie. He ate mechanically and seldom raised his eyes from his plate. Callie was hungry, but found she had difficulty swallowing as she listened to her mother's plans for their future life.

Callie, her mother said, was Becoming A Woman. She needed a Mother's Guidance. First thing tomorrow they would go shopping. Callie countered this easily with school, but there was a glint in her mother's eye that she didn't like. As soon as she could decently escape, she bolted for her room, leaving the dishes unwashed in the sink.

Maelogan had come in during dinner, and was perched on her dressing table, eating a rat. A faint odour of charred fur drifted to Callie's nostrils. Burnt hair wasn't a pleasant smell, but this evening she welcomed it as an antidote to that awful perfume of her mother's. She must have upended the bottle over herself, Callie thought. She threw herself across the bed and stared at the ceiling.

"So," said Maelogan around a bite of rat. "Your mother's come to live with you."

"How'd you know who she was?"

"Oh, I was there when she arrived. I was under the eaves, getting a spider. You have good spiders here, nice and crunchy. So are you happy to have your mother back? You don't look it, I must say."

Callie groaned. "I told you what she's like. I wasn't exaggerating, or not much, anyway. Now she says she's going to stay here. I suppose at least she didn't bring that loser Wayne with her. Apparently he's history."

"Why do you think she's come?"

Callie shrugged, as well as she could while lying down. "Says she loves us and that. I suppose Wayne dumped her."

"You don't think it might be something else?"

"What else? Summer Bay, it's hardly her kind of place. Not smart enough. No fancy shops, no art galleries, no nightlife to speak of. No famous people living down the road."

Maelogan seemed to shrug, and went back to his rat, and nothing Callie could say would draw a further word from him on the subject.

Five minutes into the science test, Callie was in her zone. She knew the work, she had the answers. Her pen raced over the paper, fluidly filling in information. She'd been so right to take the time to memorise the periodic table. A happy little smile settled over her face.

The door banged open, bouncing off the wall. All over the classroom, heads were raised; some in irritation, some with relief. A small boy stood in the doorway.

"Yes, yes, what is it?" Mr Flett barked with his customary gruff tone, bristling his huge eyebrows. "Come on, boy, speak up."

The boy blushed scarlet. "It's Calliope Jones, sir, to go to Mr Baldwin's office."

Callie gritted her teeth. She hated it when people pronounced her name to rhyme with 'dope'.

"Alright, Callie, off you go, then. See me after school about finishing the test."

Callie sighed and packed up her things. She couldn't imagine why she'd been sent for. Callie wasn't the sort of girl that got sent for to the headmaster's office. She kept her head down, kept a low profile, always had, and her work was above reproach. What was it about, she wondered uneasily. Surely nothing could have happened to Dad?

When she reached Mr Baldwin's office, though, it was all too clear what it was about. Her mother sat in Baldy's visitor chair, at her ease and displaying what Callie thought was an unseemly amount of leg for a mother, and stinking up the room with her perfume.

"Ah, Callie." Mr Baldwin seemed relieved. "Your mother is here to take you to the doctor."

"The doctor?" Callie repeated stupidly. "But I'm not sick."

Her mother smirked in an infuriating, silly-little-girl kind of way, and got up. "Come on, darling, we mustn't keep Doctor Smith waiting."

Callie compressed her lips, crossed her eyes and followed her mother out to where the Mercedes was parked right across the main driveway.

It wasn't until they were on the freeway that Callie reluctantly asked where they were going.

"We're going shopping, sweetie, and to get your hair done properly. You're much too big now to be scruffing about the way you do."

"What? But Mr Baldwin - you said a doctor."

"Oh, that was just to get you out of school. We're going to the city to get you some proper clothes, and a skincare consultation."

"But - we had a Science test. You can't just…"

"Oh, lighten up, Callie, don't be such a misery. It's not like science and all that really matters for a girl. Now a decent haircut…." She rabbitted on for several miles about haircuts and other things in which Callie had no interest. Callie sat, silently fuming. She cared about science. She cared about her position at the top of the class. She cared about her marks, and getting a scholarship one day to medical school. Okay, she wasn't that enthused about her bush of orange hair, but she was used to it, and anyway, haircuts were a Saturday thing, not a take-off-in-the-middle-of-the-school-day thing. Callie was furious, but as usual, had no way to vent her rage.

Five hours later, Callie sank exhausted into a booth in the smart, fashionable cafe her mother had chosen. Her head was spinning and she wasn't even quite sure who she was. She caught sight of her reflection in the mirror that ran along one wall. She didn't even recognise herself; she had to move before she was sure it was her reflection that she saw. Gone was the orange bush, replaced by shining, glossy waves of dark red. Her white, freckled skin had been lightly made up, blurring the freckles and accentuating her grey eyes. She was still wearing her school uniform, but that was the only thing about her that really looked like her. On both sides of her, mountainous piles of shopping bags reared up.

Callie supposed she should feel grateful. She looked fantastic, she knew, and the clothes her mother had bought her were beautiful, and the makeup lady had shown her how to do everything so that she'd be able to work the magic transformation again whenever she liked, and her hair... well, wasn't it more or less what she'd been wishing for for years? She knew she was being ungrateful, but she resented it all. Resented the high-handed way her mother had yanked her out of school. Resented that she'd swanned into her, Callie's school, and told a bare-faced lie to the principal. Resented the lost school day, a day she'd never get back, and the missed test, which she was going to have to make up at some point, and which would cause extra trouble for Mr Flett, and that was a thing that Callie never, ever did. She never caused extra trouble for anybody. That just wasn't who she was. And this, this made-up, primped, fashionable *girl*, this wasn't who she was, either. At thirteen, Callie felt she knew who she was, and if that was going to change, it ought to be her decision.

Callie didn't make the mistake of trying to explain any of this to her mother. She had written her mother off way back, and even if she hadn't, she would have done so when she'd tried to tell her about Wayne and his groping hands. She wished her mother would go away again, so they could get back to normal.

Her mother had finally stopped talking and was looking at the menu. Callie sucked in a deep breath and took the plunge.

"So, how long are you staying?"

"Staying? Whatever do you mean?"

"With us. How long are you staying here, with us?"

Her mother looked astonished. "But darling, I thought you understood. I've come home. I'm staying forever. Well, not here, of course. That rubbishy old house won't do. We'll move back to town as soon as I find something nice."

Numb with shock and horror, Callie failed to hear the rest, but it was probably just as well.

"...and she says she's staying for good, and she wants to sell this house and move back to the city! Mae, we have to DO something. Can't you get rid of her, oh, with magic or something?"

"I say, steady on there. You can't just 'get rid' of people. There would be fearful consequences. The greater the change you bring about with magic, the greater the consequences. It's like the recoil on a gun." Maelogan, since moving into the house, had discovered television, and was particularly fond of police shows, which he found hysterically funny. "If you just disappear a person, the consequences could be catastrophic."

Callie frowned. "Don't be so melodramatic. I'm not saying kill her, for heaven's sake. I mean, she is my mother. Just get rid of her. Make her go away and leave us alone."

Maelogan heaved a vast sigh and rearranged himself on the pillow. "Look, you remember what I told you back in the cave? How I could fix your problem, but there's always a price?"

"Yeah, but there wasn't."

"Oh, really? Who was that dragging you out of school today, then?"

"Well, but... hang on, are you saying...."

"Everything has consequences, don't you understand? Magic could fix your problem by providing you with a lot of money. But having that money has had consequences, hasn't it?"

"But Mum... you mean... you don't think she's here because of that, do you?"

Maelogan snorted. "What else?"

"But... Dad's her husband. She loves him, she said."

"Really? Where has she been for the last year? Was she here with him?"

"No, but...."

"She was with that other man, wasn't she?"

"Yes, but...."

"The one who hurt you. And she didn't care."

"Well, he didn't actually hurt me, he was just creepy. And it wasn't that she didn't care, she just didn't believe me."

"Hmmm."

The silence grew, and lengthened, and grew some more. Callie squirmed. It wasn't that she thought a great lot of her mother, as such, but it was hard to imagine anyone caring so much about money that she'd change her whole way of life. And yet, Callie thought, was her mother really contemplating changing her life? Was she not, rather, changing her, Callie's, and Dad's life, back to the way she liked it? She was already talking about selling their home and moving back to the city. That was the problem, and why they were having this conversation in the first place.

"So, you're saying she's just here because Dad's got a lot of money now?"

"Pretty well, yes, I should think so. I've been listening to her since she's been here. It's not difficult; she hardly ever shuts up. I've not once heard her talk about anything except things to buy."

Callie thought about that for a moment, and recognised the truth of it. Maelogan was right; her mother was all about *things*. She always had been. That had been one of the main causes of all the fights between her and Dad, the fact that Dad wasn't interested in fancy cars, or jewellery, or making a lot of money. 'Getting on,' her mother had called it. 'Being a mindless yuppie' had been Dad's term. It was small wonder they'd got divorced, Callie realised. The wonder was that they'd ever got married in the first place.

If Dad didn't have all that money, Callie supposed, her mother wouldn't be here now, making their lives a misery. Poor Dad hadn't got any writing done since she'd arrived. She was always at him, dragging him out to fancy restaurants in the city, pestering him to get haircuts and look at Better Homes and Gardens.

An idea was tickling the edges of her brain. She reached for it, but it slipped away. Don't try too hard, she thought. Just drift, like so, and....

And yes, that was it! "Mae! Mae, listen, I know what we can do!"

"Oh, yes?"

"Well, what you can do, if you want to, I mean, but look, if it's the money that's attracted her here, then if you get rid of the money, won't she go away too? Because, as you pointed out, she's a consequence of the money in the first place."

"And how do you propose to do that?"

"Well, you'd still have to do it with magic, I suppose, but it would be a small magic, wouldn't it? Because you'd actually be just putting things back the way they were supposed to be all along."

"Hmm."

"And so the consequences wouldn't be much. It's just going back to before."

"Well, not quite. I mean, that's all happened now, I can't go back and change the past. No one can do that."

"No, but you could get rid of the money, couldn't you?"

"What about the reason you had the money in the first place? This house? Your life here?"

"I don't care. It's no good here now she's come, anyway. And anyway," Callie argued, "Dad's paid off the mortgage, so the house wouldn't be affected."

"You do understand that there's no way to predict what the consequences will be?"

But Callie didn't care. She had the bit between her teeth. "Can you just find a way to get rid of the money?"

"Well, yes, I suppose so. It's quite an elegant solution. You have a good mind. But are you prepared for the consequences?"

"Meh. How bad can it be?"

It was some time before Maelogan achieved his purpose, and Callie grew extremely weary of her life. She might have got used to her mother's presence in the house, if only her mother had been willing to leave her alone, even for part of the time. But she seemed to regard Callie as a sort of plaything, a doll to be dressed up and taken out to show off with, and Callie found, as the winter dropped away and gave way to warmer weather, that her mother's company was increasingly a burden. Callie's mother required her company to go shopping. She needed Callie to accompany her to a gallery opening. The worst had been when she'd dragged her to Surfers' Paradise for a week, in the spring holidays. Can't you and Dad just go, Callie had asked. But Dad, for once, had put his foot down. The chance to be left alone for a whole week had been too much for him to resist, Callie had thought sourly. In vain had she argued that she needed to stay and look after Dad. "Nonsense," her mother had said. "Your father is perfectly able to look after himself, and he certainly doesn't need a little girl getting in his way." One of the things Callie found hardest to take about her mother was her constant failure to recognise Callie's reality, her personhood. She spoke either as if Callie was a little girl unable to understand anything more complex than a comic book, or as if she was some kind of sex object. For the trip to Surfers' Paradise, which for Callie, with her white, non-tanning, ultra-burnable skin, had been torture, she had forced her to buy a bikini that Callie hadn't even been able to look at in the shop without blushing. Honestly, she thought. Was her mum trying to promote a teen pregnancy? Callie was thirteen years old, and perhaps she was a late bloomer, but she'd have been far more comfortable in her old Speedo one-piece, with a t-shirt over the top to protect her shoulders. Or better yet, the t-shirt with her old jeans. Swimming and sunbathing all day weren't exactly a preferred option when you were a natural redhead. Callie had spent most of the week after the first day confined to their hotel room, moaning in pain and slathering on Skin Repair. She'd had to go back to school with her face all peeling, looking like she had some kind of vile disease. And then her mother had scolded her for not looking pretty.

At school she still had some measure of autonomy, but even there she was subject to interruption without notice, as her mother periodically descended with tales of spurious doctor's appointments, to drag her to stupid, pointless activities such as salon pedicures and having her 'colours' done. The consultant had said she was Winter. Callie had certainly felt very wintry that day.

Callie stayed late at the library, looking up material for her History project, and it was full dark by the time she coasted down the long hill. She tossed her backpack in the hall and walked singing into the kitchen. The long ride in the gathering dark had energised her, and she was looking forward to trying out a new variation on her usual curry. It was a recipe the new girl, Aparna Patel, had given her. Callie's mother frequently complained about Callie's plain cooking, but as her complaints never seemed to inspire any more practical contribution than buying jars of expensive pâté, they had faded into the background noise of Callie's life. Nevertheless, Callie felt, she ought to make some effort towards more sophisticated cuisine. It might appease her enough that she'd leave Dad alone for once.

There were voices coming from the sitting room, but Callie tuned them out and got on with chopping vegetables and slicing some fillet steak for Maelogan, who presently flew in through the open window and settled on the counter.

"You're getting too big to do that, Mae. Fly in fast like that. Soon you won't fit. I'll come home and find you wedged in the window with your bum hanging out, like Winnie the Pooh."

"Winnie who? Do you mean that warrior chap?" Maelogan had loved hearing about the Second World War, although Callie wasn't sure how clearly he understood it; he persisted in viewing Churchill as a great warrior, sort of a latter-day Alexander the Great. It wasn't worth arguing about it yet again. She put his metal plate of meat out of the way, in the corner of the counter, trying to keep some space for a preparation surface. "I'm going to have to put this on the floor for you soon, the way you're growing."

Maelogan paid no attention, being fully occupied in breathing flame over his dinner, crisping it to the particular degree of charred outside, raw inside, that he favoured. Really,

Callie thought, it was just like the steak had been at that pretentious restaurant Mum had dragged them to the previous week. Perhaps she ought to let Maelogan cook their food; there might be fewer complaints. She sniggered.

Callie's mother teetered into the kitchen on her stiletto heels. Second martini, Callie thought. There was just the faintest wobble about the ankles, which suggested she'd had more than one, but not as many as three, because her makeup was still immaculate and there were no frown lines to be seen. Callie sighed. She hoped Mum wasn't going to hang around the kitchen trying to have another one of those 'mother-daughter' talks. She'd had those up to here already. She started to unpack the spices she'd bought on the way home onto the kitchen table.

"There you are, darling!" Quick as a flash, Mum noticed I was here, Callie thought sourly.

"Yes, Mum, here I am."

"How was school?"

For God's sake, Callie wanted to say, you ask that every single day, and every single day I say it was fine. "Excellent," she said. "Wonderful, divine, absolutely spiffing, what?" Sometimes the temptation to take the piss was just too strong to be denied. She knew it would have not the slightest impact on her mother, who had room in her head for only one idea at a time, and if she was on her second martini, perhaps not even that.

"I came in," said her mother, "to tell you we have a guest for dinner. So do try to make something a bit more exciting than chops, can you, sweetie?"

Damn, thought Callie. Damn, damn, double damn. Bugger. She knew a guest meant she'd be expected to hang about all night serving coffee and being seen and not heard. She and Maelogan had been planning a moonlight walk along the beach after dinner. It was a full moon, and a lovely clear night.

Perhaps she could pretend she had urgent homework and sneak out the back door.

The next moment, though, she realised that was the least of her worries as her mother let out a shriek and froze into a melodramatic pose, one outstretched arm pointing dramatically at Maelogan, who had finished his meal and was perched on the counter, grooming his whiskers. "WHAT!" she screeched, "is THAT!"

Callie's mind whirled in panic. She didn't know whether to be more annoyed at her mother or at Maelogan. He'd been so positive that people couldn't see him, or couldn't see his 'true nature', whatever that meant, that she'd gradually become accustomed to him being about the house in plain sight. Dad never noticed anything anyway, and her mother was generally focussed on herself with the concentration of a brain surgeon performing a ground-breaking new operation.

"It's, um, it's a... um...."

"Callie, you know I cannot BEAR cats. Where on earth did it come from?"

Cats? Was that what he'd meant about his true nature? Would people just see him as a cat?

"Um... in the window...."

"Well it can just go OUT the window again. Shoo!" She grabbed a tea towel and flapped it ineffectually at Maelogan from the other side of the kitchen. "Vile thing. Get out, shoo!"

Maelogan, catching Callie's frantic, agonised glance, launched himself from the windowsill and flew off. Callie's mother rushed to the window and slammed it shut. "That settles it. We must have screens installed. The bugs are bad enough, but if we're going to have rabid strays coming in every five minutes it just isn't safe."

Dinner was vile, although Aparna's curry

recipe was delicious. The guest turned out to be a flashy type from some financial planning company. Callie thought he looked like a boat salesman, with his orange tan, slightly too long hair and shiny brass buttons. Why did all her mother's friends have to be so sketchy, she wondered. Perhaps only the sketchy ones could put up with her mother, she answered herself. There had to be a lot in that. Callie herself couldn't put up with her, after all.

The conversation over dinner was excruciatingly dull. It seemed to be all about money and investments and something called 'futures'. Once she was sure she wasn't going to be required to say anything, Callie tuned it out. At the other end of the table, her father seemed to have had the same idea, and was shovelling in his dinner and staring out the window. From time to time he detected a sharp, interrogatory note in his wife's voice and roused himself to utter a few vaguely placatory words of agreement. Callie's mother kept pouring more wine, and seemed to be flirting with the boat guy, whose name, apparently was Tod. How bogus could one person be, thought Callie. Tod, for God's sake. She escaped as early as she could decently manage, using a fictional maths test as her excuse. All the way upstairs, she could hear her mother's patronising laughter. As if wanting to be a doctor was somehow silly.

Callie shook her shoulders. What was she thinking, letting her mother get to her? She didn't matter. She was just rattled, she decided, from her mother seeing Maelogan. For a horrible second she'd thought... but there; he'd been right after all. All her mother had seen had been a scruffy stray cat.

In her room, Maelogan was curled on the end of her bed. Lucky she'd left the window open, Callie thought, but soon it would be winter. She couldn't have it opened right up all the time then. Four inches was supposed to be enough for a cat, but Maelogan was a lot bigger than a cat now. He was almost as big as a Labrador, she realised with surprise. When had that happened?

"So listen," she began. "Mum saw you tonight."

Maelogan sneered. Of course he didn't really sneer, not like a human would, but when you hung out with someone all the time you got to be able to read their facial expressions, and he had this kind of thing he did with his whiskers that denoted contempt.

"I could hardly miss that, Callie. The way she was shrieking, I should think everyone in the country knew it."

Callie blushed. Her mother was loud, no one knew that better than she did, but suddenly she realised she was different in other ways, too. Her mother was a different kind of person than Dad. Not just flashier and more painted, but more... coarse, somehow. Dad was oblivious half the time, true, but when he did surface, he wasn't just all about himself. If he thought about you at all, he thought about you as a real person. If you asked him for something you wanted, he'd get it for you if he possibly could. Or if he couldn't, he'd tell you why. He'd admit he didn't have the money or whatever. He wouldn't go on at you for wanting the wrong things. Authentic, that was what Dad was, and her mother was somehow not authentic, somehow counterfeit. It came to Callie all at once, in a hot rush of misery, that she was ashamed of her mother.

Wrestling with this new thought, which made her violently resentful, uncomfortable and embarrassed all at the same time, Callie did not immediately register the fact that Maelogan was still talking.

"... and bones. A bone would be nice once in a while."

"Bones? What bones?"

"Stupid girl. The bones you will be able to get for me, of course, when I am established as the house dog."

"You never said you wanted bones. I could

get you bones now."

Maelogan sighed. "People are starting to see me now. Your mother has already seen me, and your father will too. As will anyone else who comes here. As I seem to be rather larger than before, and as your mother obviously has an aversion to cats, we should present me as a dog. A 'cover story', you see, as they have in the stories in the magic box."

"It's called a television, Mae. It's not magic, I've told you and told you."

Maelogan dismissed the distinction with an airy wave of his plumed tail. "Tomorrow I shall meet you just on the other side of the hill, and accompany you, on foot, back to the house. Anyone who looks out of a window will see a large, yellow dog."

"How d'you know what they'll see? Mum saw a cat tonight."

"She was full of metheglyn. I was on the counter; she saw what she expected to see.

When I'm running along behind your bicycle machine, she'll see a dog."

That seemed reasonable, Callie supposed. Up to a point.

"But why do it at all? Why not just go on the way we are? I can get you a bone if you want a bone, heavens, I've only got to buy it at the butcher. This way, there's... there's risk. Don't you see? There's no way Mum will let me keep a dog. And where would I say I got it?"

"You say whatever you think will have the best effect, of course. If it's your mother, you want to say the dog's very expensive and prestigious. If it's your father, I should think saying you'd rescued a starving stray would go down well. Make sure they're not together when you talk to them, and you can use both stories."

Callie snorted. "That would be so great, wouldn't it. Honestly Mae, don't you think people talk to each other? How awkward would it be when they found out? A, I wouldn't be allowed to keep the dog, and B, they'd never believe anything I said again. And anyway, I don't want to lie to Dad. I've never lied to Dad. He doesn't lie to me. We just don't tell lies."

"Just your father? You don't mind lying to your mother?"

Callie flushed scarlet. She didn't mind at all, she realised, because her mother didn't count. She'd written her mother off as really mattering back when she'd been, what, eight? Because her mother never seemed to see any value in her, Callie, as she was - at eight she'd been something to dress up in pretty frocks and boast about to her friends, and Callie, with her skinned knees, wild fuzzy hair and missing front tooth which always seemed to happen the day before the school photo, was not part of that picture. But wasn't that exactly what she, Callie, had done? She hadn't mattered to her mother, and so she had responded by making her mother not matter to her. And she'd never, ever reconsidered her decision.

In her own way, she was as bad as her mother.

"Look," she began, "I really don't want to lie to either of them. I'm just not a lying person," she went on, adding a truth to the half-truth. "Can't we just... I don't know, do something else?"

"Well, I don't know what," said Maelogan, "you humans never have anything else in the house besides cats and dogs."

"Dad," began Callie the following Saturday, "I really want a dog. Can I get a dog?" Directness was always best with her father; apart from anything else, if you tried to lead up to anything in a more subtle way, he was likely to vague out before you got to what you were leading up to. She'd waited until her mother was out of the house to bring up the subject. If Dad said yes, it would be a done deal and there would be nothing her mother could do. If Dad said no, she could work on persuading him, but as long as her mother was out of the picture she had a better chance of success.

Dad looked at her over the tops of his glasses. There had been a steady tapping of the keyboard for a couple of hours, and she'd just brought him in a cup of coffee, so conditions were as nearly optimal as they could be.

"A dog? That's very sudden, isn't it? You've never wanted a dog before. What's brought this on?"

"Dad, I so, so want a dog. Please can I? I can get one free. And I have wanted one before. I wanted one when I was eight, and Mum said no." Shit, shit, shit. She'd blurted that out as soon as she'd remembered it, and now she'd brought Mum into the picture when that had been the very thing she'd wanted at all costs to avoid. She cast about for damage control. Ah, yes. "She said it would wreck the carpets, we had that white carpet, remember? But here we've got the wood floors, so it wouldn't matter."

"Oh well," said her father vaguely, glancing back at his computer screen, "as long as you take care of it yourself, I don't see why not. What sort of dog?"

Callie, momentarily stumped, opted for her trump card. "A homeless one. He's got nowhere else to go, and they only keep them eight days if they're taken to the pound, then they kill them." That ought to distract him; Dad was always far more interested in real stuff than appearances. Predictably, he beamed with pride.

"You're a good girl, Callie. Not a shallow or selfish bone in your body. Let me just finish this chapter and I'll drive you in to pick him up. You'll be wanting some things from the supermarket for him too, I suppose."

Damn. She hadn't seen that coming. Now what could she - ah, yes. "Not really Dad, he's been accustomed to a raw diet, you know, they call it Barf - bones and raw food - so I'll only need meat from the butcher, and I can pick that up on the way there."

"But won't you need, oh, a basket? And toys and things?"

"I want him to sleep on my bed. Don't tell Mum, okay? And I've already got tennis balls, from before... anyway, I've got at least six of those. He'll be fine. Anything else I can get on the way home from school on Monday. I don't want to take you away from your book, not when it's going so well." That's got him. Look at him, he's desperate to get back to it.

"Oh, well, you know best," said her father, his mind already ninety percent back with Detective Inspector Fanshawe.

Callie was out the door in a flash, running for her bicycle with her father's last words, "Don't you think we should check with your mother..." conveniently unheard, or nearly unheard, anyway - as good as unheard, she told herself.

Maelogan met her as arranged, just the other

side of the top of the hill, swooping out of the sky like a magpie in spring. The morning sun glistened off his golden scales, and he was, thought Callie fondly, more beautiful than any creature she'd ever seen. He didn't give her any time to admire him, though.

"Right, back on your machine, let's go. You go ahead and I'll run along behind, like we saw on the magic box."

"What's the hurry? We could walk back."

"I don't want anyone seeing me out here. The more context there is, the thicker the expectations, you see, and it's easier to do the glamour I'll need."

"Glamour?" Callie thought he was quite glamorous enough. "Wasn't the whole point of pretending to be a dog not to be glamorous?"

"Stupid girl. The glamour I must cast, of course, so that I will be seen as a dog. It's a kind of spell."

"What, wait, will I see you as a dog too?"

"I think that would be safest, don't you? Best if you see what everyone else sees."

"Well go on, then, what are you waiting for?"

"Just a second, don't rush me." Maelogan squatted down in the road and assumed an air of intense concentration. Gradually the air around him started to shimmer, and ratty grey fur sprouted in clumps, spreading until it completely obscured his golden scales. Callie watched in fascination as his wings shrank away to nothing and his emerald eyes deepened to a rich brown. Finally, a skinny, scruffy hound crouched in the dirt before her. It looked a bit like a greyhound, but with long, shaggy fur. It stood up, its head reaching to her waist.

"Good grief! D'you think you're tall enough?"

"Conservation of mass, girl. The extra weight had to go somewhere."

"Mum's going to freak. Literally freak. Hey,

will they be able to hear you talking?"

"Not at all. That's inside your mind, you hear that. And remember, you can talk to me that way, too. You don't need to talk out loud - just think towards me, I'll hear you."

"Ewww, you're reading my mind?"

"Certainly not; that would be improper, and boring besides. When you think on purpose for me to hear, that only will I hear."

"But you could, then? Read someone's mind?" Why was she only now asking these things, Callie wondered. She supposed the shock of seeing Maelogan transform like that had activated some core of belief in things she'd never believed in that had remained untouched by the fact of Mae himself, or the money, which after all might have been a coincidence, or dowsing or something. She supposed one could locate gold by dowsing or something similar. After all, it had a lot more presence than water.

The effect produced on Mrs Jones by finding, on her return from the hairdresser, a three-foot-tall hound in residence was no disappointment to anybody. In fact, it could hardly have been overlooked even if anyone had wanted to, as she spent the ensuing three hours describing it, at length and in detail, to her husband. Poor Dad, thought Callie. There goes his output for the day.

Dad remained staunchly inflexible, repeating to every demand the unshakeable argument, "But I already told her she could." Presently, a row of massive proportions erupted. Really, it was quite like the old days, back in Double Bay. Callie and Maelogan retreated to the beach cave.

Over the next few weeks, everyone except Mrs Jones adjusted to Maelogan's presence in the house. Maelogan was quiet, didn't bark, didn't destroy anything, and waited politely at the back door to be let out. He didn't even shed hair, which was not surprising to Callie, as she knew the fur was an illusion, but impressed her father no end when it was pointed out to him. This had been in response to a complaint by Callie's mother that everything was covered in dog hair, and a challenge by Callie to find one single hair. Mrs Jones had been unable to do so, and had taken refuge in the vodka bottle, throwing out small, bitter remarks for the rest of the evening, just in case, Callie thought, anyone might have been going to relax. Gradually, however, her grumbling subsided as she was forced to admit that Maelogan made no extra work, cost very little to feed and in general gave no trouble.

It was not until early September that the crunch came. Callie arrived home from school one afternoon to find her parents going at it hammer and tongs, with her mother in a state verging on hysteria. Her first impulse was to get out of her school uniform and escape to the beach at the double, but Maelogan, curled up on the sofa, displayed a strange reluctance to move, even when she tugged on the red leather collar she'd bought him. There had been quite an argument over that collar, but Maelogan had acquiesced in the end, when Callie had pointed out to him how handsome and distinguished it made him look, and how it added verisimilitude to his disguise.

"Come on, Mae," hissed Callie, desperately wanting to get away from the shouting and rowing, which she'd never been able to bear.

Maelogan dug in his paws and hunkered down on the sofa, refusing to move. And faintly, in a corner of Callie's mind, came the whispered "I think this is it."

"It? What it?" Callie had blurted before she remembered she shouldn't have spoken out loud. "What is wrong with you?" she continued, to cover up her slip.

"It. The getting rid of the money thing. This fight started because your father got a letter from his bank. He says all his money is gone."

Callie felt the blood drain from her face. It

had all seemed so simple in the planning. Get rid of the money, and her mother would bugger off back to Double Bay or wherever. The reality was much, much more scary. What if she didn't bugger off? What if now they would have no money *and* Callie's mum? She wanted to throw up. Why couldn't she have left well enough alone, or found another way, or something? She hadn't counted on things being like this every day.

Presently Callie's mother went out, jumped into her car and stormed off, spraying gravel, and Dad sank down into an armchair, taking off his glasses and rubbing his temples as he always did when one of his headaches was coming on.

Over the course of the evening and many cups of coffee made by Callie on the flash espresso machine, the story emerged. Dad had received a letter from the bank in that afternoon's post, informing him that the cheque he'd written to pay the credit card account had bounced. He had immediately cancelled the card, which was still being used by her mother, but of more concern was the fact that when he had accessed his investment account to transfer funds to the current account to pay the bill, it had come up empty.

At this point, Dad went on after Callie had fetched him another espresso, an ice pack for his head and some aspirin, he had become aware that something was very, very wrong, and had called Tod Benham.

Callie shook her head. "Tod who?"

"Benham, Tod Benham. You remember him, that friend of your mother's. He came to dinner once. She was very keen that I buy into his investment portfolio. It was supposed to pay huge dividends, and your mother felt I wasn't making the best use of our investment funds...."

Callie frowned. "But who is he? I mean, does he work for the stock market or something?" Callie had a very hazy idea of how financial things worked.

"Not exactly," said Dad. "He represented a group of private investors. They were taking advantage of a niche in the futures market."

"What does that even mean?" asked Callie. She'd never heard of a futures market, but she had a very bad feeling about it.

Dad rubbed his temples again. When he lifted his head, his expression was rueful. "I'm sorry, Callie, I don't understand it myself. Benham was supposed to be such a financial whiz-kid, I just more or less accepted his advice. I've never been very clever about money, you know."

Callie did know; no one better. Their life together had made it painfully clear. If anyone understood how money, or anything else practical, worked in this family, it was she.

"So what does this Tod guy say now? Maybe it's a mistake or something?"

"I can't get him on the phone. It seems his office number's been disconnected."

"His mobile?"

Dad looked out the window, obviously mustering his courage.

"That's been disconnected too."

Callie put it all together much more easily than her father had done. Having more or less denied her imagination for most of her life, she lacked the ordinary person's ability to dress up unpalatable facts.

"He's done a runner. Dad, he's cleaned you out, probably other people too, and shot off."

Dad didn't appear to be able to speak, and Callie felt a bit sorry to have been so blunt. She patted his shoulder awkwardly. "Don't worry, Dad, it'll be ok. We weren't really cut out to be rich people, you and me, anyway, were we?"

"But what are we going to do? That money was going to put you through university, and now..." He was dithering, she realised. He needed someone to take the reins. As she had done so many times before, Callie Jones, aged thirteen and a half, squared her shoulders and stepped up.

"Dad, you know perfectly well I'll get a scholarship. That's always been the plan. And if I don't, well, I'll just have to work my way through. People do, you know. As for what we're going to do now, well first thing tomorrow, you'll report him to the police or whoever. And then, well, we'll just go on living. It's not so bad, Dad, things might be a bit tight for a while, but you've got your royalties and you've nearly finished your new book, haven't you, and then the house is paid for. We'll be fine." She forced a confident smile, and went to the kitchen to see about dinner.

Callie's mother did not return for dinner, and Callie and her father sat down to a hastily scratched-together meal of macaroni cheese and salad. After that, Callie saw her father, who had not just the usual sort but one of his really bad headaches, off to bed with a rare sleeping pill.

Later, in her room, Callie and Maelogan came as close as they had ever been to quarrelling.

"Stop snivelling, girl. You know I can't abide it."

"I am not snivelling. I'm just saying. It was a stupid idea, getting rid of the money. Look at the state Dad's in. How can he write his book when he's all worried? How can he do anything? You saw what he was like, and he's got one of his migraines. It was better before we messed with it. At least we didn't have her all over us."

"And soon you won't have her all over you again. That was the whole point, remember?"

"But what if she doesn't go? She said she was back for good, because she loves Dad."

Maelogan was so irritated that he allowed his disguise spell to slip, revealing a flash of golden scales. "Whatever, bitch." He turned his back pointedly and curled himself into a ball.

"Mae! That's so rude! And since when do you use that kind of expression?"

"I heard it on the magic box."

It was not until long past eleven that Callie heard her mother's car pull into the driveway. She lay in the dark and listened to the uneven footsteps coming up the stairs, and a small crash and muffled swearing as her mother staggered against the wall. She must have been drinking a lot, Callie thought, even for her. She stretched her ears, listening as hard as she could, but didn't hear anything from her parents' room except a few muffled thuds. Dad would be out for the count after taking one of his migraine pills. Probably just as well, she thought. They'd all had enough screaming for one day. The thudding sounds continued, and she heard drawers opening and closing. What on earth was her mother doing? Surely she couldn't be cleaning out her wardrobe at this time of night?

The muffled banging didn't let up, and Callie drifted into a troubled and restless sleep where baffling, unpleasant dream fragments succeeded each other in an anxious cascade. She woke suddenly in the small hours, her heart pounding, her body flushed with adrenaline.

Sitting up and pushing her hands through her hair, Callie tried to make sense of why she'd woken with such a start. The house was quiet, Maelogan curled at her feet, breathing evenly and occasionally letting out a wisp of steam, his dragon snore. Had she had a bad dream? She tried to push her consciousness back into the recent past, but all she could remember of it was a feeling of confusion and loss, something heavy being dragged and the sound of car doors slamming. Straining her ears now, she caught the distinctive sound of gears shifting down on the hill. Someone was up early, she thought, wondering who had driven past their isolated house at five in the morning. She drifted back into an uneasy doze, but couldn't get properly back to sleep, and when the heaviness leached out of the sky and the first magpie loosed its full-throated exultation, she got up and went downstairs.

No wonder she'd slept badly, she realised as she saw the front door swinging open. She must have had some dim awareness in her sleep that all wasn't right with the house, that it wasn't properly shut up for the night. Callie had developed the habit of checking round last thing, seeing that the doors were locked for the night and everything in its place. A tidy house meant there'd be no unexpected problems to delay her in the morning. The front door, standing wide to the night, was an affront to her habit of orderliness, and she went to close it, tutting to herself at her mother's slovenly ways. She'd been drinking, Callie supposed, and had come in in a state. God knew where she'd left the car; probably in the middle of Callie's tiny, carefully mown lawn. She hoped the box seedlings she'd planted along the front hadn't been flattened. But when she poked her head out, her mother's car was nowhere to be seen.

Overhead, footsteps crossed the floor and she heard the toilet flush. Dad was up, ready to start his writing day. She went to start a pot of coffee for him. But Dad was downstairs in much less than his usual twenty minutes, still in his robe and with his hair poking out every which way. It wanted cutting dreadfully, she noticed with a pang of guilt. She should have reminded him.

"Morning, Dad. Coffee's on."

But Callie's father was strangely uninterested in coffee, which at this early hour suggested some great emergency.

"Callie, did your mother say anything to you last night?"

"No Dad, she hadn't got back when I went to bed. I heard her come in, but I didn't get up. Is everything okay?"

Dad sank down into a chair, rested his elbows on the kitchen table and pushed his hands into his disorderly hair, staring at the table surface as if it held some desperately important piece of information. He didn't speak right away, and there was time for the coffee machine to finish, and for Callie to pour his coffee, adding just a tiny smidgin of milk the way he liked it. She slid it in front of him and sat down with her own weak, heavily-sugared cappuccino. Callie had acquired the coffee habit, despite not liking the taste very much, when they'd got the big fancy espresso machine, because Dad had been so thrilled with it and she'd wanted to increase his enjoyment by letting him share it. She'd have this quiet half hour with him before starting her day; she had a couple of hours in hand before she needed to leave for school. She often sat with him so, he drinking his first and she her only coffee of the day. It was their time, even now that her mother was back. A small pleasure she hadn't been able to spoil, Callie caught herself thinking, and was a little shocked at herself.

"She's gone, Callie. Your mother's gone."

Reacting to his miserable tone, about to agree sympathetically, Callie caught herself, replaying the words to her unbelieving mind.

"What d'you mean, gone? I heard her come in last night."

"She's gone. She said... well, never mind that. She's left us again. Callie, I'm so sorry."

Callie couldn't process it.

"But why?" She asked the question, knowing deep down why, but unable to believe that even her mother would be so shallow as to go the very same day the money ran out.

Her father drew in a long, shaky breath and sighed. He seemed unable to meet her eyes.

"I was a big disappointment to her, you know. When we married... she knew I was a writer, but she expected me to be like Stephen King, or one of those people. Rich, famous...."

"You are famous, Dad. Lots of people read your books. You support us by it, for heaven's sake."

"Not very adequately. Look at this house. Until you found that gold nugget last year, we were on our uppers. You know we were, Callie, we had to get all your school uniforms from the second-hand shop."

"Yeah, well uniforms are expensive, aren't they, way more expensive than normal clothes. Anyway, who cares? We always had a roof over our heads, we always had enough to eat. You've looked after us really well, Dad, always. I was so happy...." She bit off her sentence before the terrible words, 'until she came' slipped out. Her father reached out and gripped her hand without speaking. They sat, holding hands, while the sun rose and light gilded the shabby kitchen.

ಬPART IIIಚಿ

In the weeks that followed, information emerged, each new discovery slotting into the picture Callie was building up of what had really been going on in her family. It seemed her mother had known Tod Benham much, much better than had appeared to be the case; they were, in fact, now in Surfers' Paradise together. They had met there on that dreadful holiday; while Callie had been nursing her sunburn in the hotel room, her mother had been getting acquainted with her new conquest around the hotel pool.

This, as it now appeared, close friendship had predated Callie's father's investment in Tod's dodgy company by quite some time.

The police were sympathetic, but ultimately unhelpful. It was, evidently, not a matter for the police. The Australian Securities and Investments Commission, although interested, eventually decided there was nothing that could be done. Tod Benham, sketchy though he undoubtedly was, was also clever, and had known what he was doing to a 'T'. The provision for management fees in the contract Callie's father had signed left him plenty of 'wriggle room' and he was now living happily in Surfers' Paradise, a wealthy man.

After her father's initial depression at being left a second time, he cheered up wonderfully. Not being constantly nagged and told he wasn't good enough, Callie suspected, was a marvellous tonic, much better for him really than having lots of money. Things were a little tight until the quarterly royalties came in, but Callie had got into the habit of socking away a little of the housekeeping money each week and by the time her mother had left, her secret slush fund had contained twelve hundred and eighty-seven dollars, which was more than enough to cover the groceries and necessary items in those first weeks, and once the royalty cheque did come, Callie's father was gratified to realise that now that there were no house payments to be made, he could easily live on his royalties. This realisation, a rare and beautiful one for any writer, caused him to drift about in a soft glow of happiness that never quite wore off.

Their income was further supplemented before long. Callie, who had never forgotten her own unhappiness when she first went to Summer Bay High, had made friends with the new girl on general principle, and as their friendship deepened it emerged that Aparna's father was a lawyer in the city, returning home to his family each weekend. A closer acquaintance between the two families revealed that Callie's father was now able to pursue her mother for child support payments, as her wealth, in her joint holdings with Benham, now so far exceeded his. "Hoist with her own petard, what?" chortled the plump and amiable Mr Patel, at one of the joint family dinners that had become a regular event.

Callie settled back into the happy, placid life she'd loved so well before her mother's advent. Weeks, then months, slipped by, their passing marked only by the tests in which Callie regularly came top, although she had to work a little harder now to beat her new friend. Aparna's bent was more for English and languages, though, where Callie was at her strongest with Science and Maths, so their competition remained amiable, each besting the other in her strong subjects. They planned to share an apartment at university, where Callie would do Medicine and Aparna would do Law.

"It's really all turned out for the best," Callie said dreamily as she sat with Maelogan on the cliff's edge, looking out to sea. "There was a time I thought everything was ruined, but it's all come right."

"So, you think you'll be alright now?" asked Maelogan lazily.

"Oh yes, I think so, don't you? Dad's happy, I'm happy, the house is safe, everything's going to be fine. Everything is fine."

"Well that's a good thing," said Maelogan, "because I shall be leaving soon."

"Mae! You can't!"

"I must, I'm afraid. It's time for me to move on."

"What, like Mary Poppins? You can't go. You were lonely before, you know you were. You said so."

Maelogan sighed. "I heard a rumour of dragons, somewhere west of here. I need to find them, if it's true. My own kind, Callie. A mate, and eggs... I have to go."

Callie couldn't speak for a while. Her throat hurt, and her vision was suddenly blurry.

"But you're my best friend, Mae. What will I do?"

"Oh, child. It was never going to be forever. Nothing is, don't you see? All of life is change. When we stop changing, we die. You'll have your life, you'll live your dreams, and now, well, I need to live mine."

He stood, in the early morning sunshine, seeming suddenly much larger. When had that happened, Callie wondered. He was almost... and as he let the glamour fall away, the shaggy grey fur turning to wisps of mist and vanishing on the breeze, and stood revealed in shining gold, Callie's breath caught in her throat with awe and wonder. Now the size of a pony, he was a creature of legend and imagination, an old tapestry come to life. As he spread his wings, their gold glistening in the sun, tears came to her eyes, not selfish tears of loss, but the tears of wonder that are humanity's ultimate tribute to pure beauty.

"Farewell, Callie," he said, his tones oddly

formal. "My blessing upon thee and thine. May thy days be long and thy harvests bountiful."

Callie hugged him once, fiercely. "I hope you find the other dragons, Mae. I hope you find everything you're looking for. Come back and see me, won't you?"

Maelogan didn't answer. Then his whiskers quirked in amusement. "Live long and prosper," he said, and launched himself off the cliff's edge, diving briefly to fill his wings and then soaring gloriously above her head.

"What - that's from that old show-"

Maelogan circled her three times in farewell, and as he turned inland and headed west, his voice came faintly back to her, drifting on the wind.

"I heard it on the magic box...."

THE END

Also by Tabitha Ormiston-Smith

NOVELS

Dance of Chaos: Lazy, frivolous, conceited and totally self-centred, Fiona MacDougall is not an asset to the workforce. When she applies for a transfer to the Infotech department of her company, she does so only in order to get an afternoon off work.

Can she succeed in her challenging new job?

Can she save her little brother from the consequences of his evil deeds?

Will Moses do something embarrassing to the vicar's leg again?

Gift of Continence: With the perfect wedding dress, what can go wrong? A great deal, as Fiona McDougall rapidly discovers. From the wedding from hell onwards, Fiona successively discovers that her new husband is stingy, bad-tempered and an adulterer.

King's Ransom: What really went on back in 1193? Was Richard Lionheart really the hero we think? Was John really that bad? And who was Robin Hood, no really, who was he?

COLLECTION

Once Upon A Dragon: Collected short fiction. A non-themed, cross-genre collection of short fiction, including fantasy, science fiction and horror as well as general fiction.

NOVELLAS

Melanie's Diary: Melanie's life is out of control. Her status-hungry parents have forced her grandmother into a home, and she's under siege from the school bully. But things are going to get a lot worse before they get better...

Dancing Feet: Ashley is devastated when her widowed father returns from his business trip with a new wife and her two daughters in tow. Pushed to one side by the interlopers, can she make a new life for herself?

Operation Tomcat (Operation Tomcat Book 1): Left almost penniless after divorcing her cheating husband, Tammy moves to the country to reinvent her life. But life in a country town isn't as simple as it looks....

Operation Camilla (Operation Tomcat Book 2): A sleazy solicitor hacks into a dating website in order to boost his failing family law practice. But he doesn't count on Tom....

Operation Badger (Operation Tomcat Book 3): Detective Senior Constable Ben Jackson is handsome, kind, diligent, dedicated and a total mensch. He's also as thick as two planks.

His girlfriend, Tammy, is clever as anything, but sillier than a wet hen.

And then there is Tom. Tom is a cat.

NON-FICTION

Grammar Without Tears: Historical and fictional characters explain common grammatical errors in a funny-as-hell book that will forever change the way you see grammar.

Fifty Shades of Grammar: Everyone, it's said, has one book inside him, but getting it out can be problematical. Perhaps you can't English very well, or you work long hours and just don't have time, or you started writing and then got stuck? Fear not, for help is at hand.

Packed with friendly, no-nonsense advice, Fifty Shades of Grammar will answer all those questions you were too afraid to ask. From sentence structure to punctuation, from setting up your workspace to support your efforts to overcoming the dreaded 'writer's block', from traps and pitfalls to avoid to editing, the problems faced by the novice writer are clearly addressed – and with LOLCATS!

With this book at your side, the only variables will be your talent and your commitment.